PRAISE FOR *YOU CRUSHED IT*

"Heartache, psychic tailspins, so-hip-it-hurts scenesters, and the pursuit of the ever-elusive punchline—*You Crushed It* has all the makings of a future classic. Baril Guérard and Smith are a literary pairing destined for greatness." — Jean Marc Ah-Sen, author of *Kilworthy Tanner*

"Despite being a story set in the world of stand-up comedy, *You Crushed It* is melancholy in the best way. A page-turner fairy tale for grown-ups—told from the most unique perspective and in full control of its brilliantly ambitious timeline—it is a tale of love, success, and betrayal. What I liked the most about it, however, was its intimacy that turned us, readers, into witnesses of an incredibly nuanced portrayal of a heartbreak." — Jowita Bydlowska, author of *Monster*

You Crushed It

Jean-Philippe Baril Guérard

Translated by Neil Smith

LITERATURE IN TRANSLATION SERIES
BOOK*HUG PRESS
TORONTO 2025

FIRST ENGLISH EDITION
Original text © 2021 by Jean-Philippe Baril Guérard
Originally published as *Haute démolition* © 2021 by Les Éditions de Ta Mère
English translation © 2025 by Neil Smith

Library and Archives Canada Cataloguing in Publication

Title: You crushed it / Jean-Philippe Baril Guérard ; translated by Neil Smith.
Other titles: Haute démolition. English
Names: Baril Guérard, Jean-Philippe, 1988- author. | Smith, Neil, 1964- translator.
Series: Literature in translation series.
Description: First English edition. | Series statement: Literature in translation series | Translation of: Haute démolition. | In English, translated from the French.
Identifiers: Canadiana (print) 2024052425X | Canadiana (ebook) 2024052635X
  ISBN 9781771669313 (softcover)
  ISBN 9781771669320 (EPUB)
Subjects: LCGFT: Novels.
Classification: LCC PS8603.A73545 H3813 2025 | DDC C843/.6—dc23

The production of this book was made possible through the generous assistance of the Canada Council for the Arts and the Ontario Arts Council. Book*hug Press also acknowledges the support of the Government of Canada through the Canada Book Fund and the Government of Ontario through the Ontario Book Publishing Tax Credit and the Ontario Book Fund.

Book*hug Press acknowledges that the land on which it operates is the traditional territory of many nations, including the Mississaugas of the Credit, the Anishnabeg, the Chippewa, the Haudenosaunee, and the Wendat peoples. We also recognize the enduring presence of many diverse First Nations, Inuit, and Métis peoples and are grateful for the opportunity to meet and work on this territory.

YOU TOLD YOURSELF NOTHING BAD COULD HAPPEN. You were warm and comfy in a taxi, your face pressed against the window. Still, you had to hold back from telling the driver to pull over and let you out so you could walk home and fall face-first into bed.

You didn't think you looked presentable enough to go to some party. You smelled like a guy who didn't give a fuck: a mix of cigarettes, three pints of red ale, and the sweat of a pig being led to slaughter, which you always secrete a few minutes before you go onstage and which stays stuck to your skin for the rest of the night.

The show had worn you out. You weren't sure you had the energy to put on a happy face and go fight for attention at a party. But Sam looked away from the road to say, almost threateningly, "You're not bailing on me, are you?"

To have fun at a party, Sam didn't need you, but he planned ahead. He wanted to be sure you'd be close at hand if he didn't find anyone interesting enough to occupy his time. A backup plan so he wouldn't be the dude in the corner alone knocking back his beer and trying to hide that he felt like a little kid lost at the mall.

"No, course not," you muttered. You couldn't hide a yawn, though. Sam took a warm Guru out of his backpack, tossed it to you. You didn't act fast enough, and the can hit you on the cheek, then fell on the seat.

"You're a fucking moron," you said.

"Work on your reflexes, bro." Sam barked a laugh, then

leaned his forehead back on the greasy mark he'd left on the window of the cab.

It'd been barely an hour since you and Sam had gotten offstage. An okay gig. A cold, noisy house, a screwy lineup, a lame emcee, and you were tired, but you'd been present at least, a hundred per cent present despite the conditions, and people laughed and maybe managed to enjoy life a little, so you didn't totally bomb. Nothing embarrassing went down, and you even got big applause when you did your bit on kindergarten class reunions. The crowd was enthusiastic, but just nothing to write home about. You told yourself not to worry. You couldn't kill every night. You got what you wanted at least: your set went over better than Sam's. That was all that mattered.

You often find Sam's routines predictable. His set-ups are so obvious that you see his punchlines coming from a mile away. He also has an unhealthy obsession with high school. Almost all his jokes involve some anecdote about gym class or a house party or necking at the lockers, like his social life peaked at sixteen. And he always closes with a callback that doesn't add much and isn't very clever (though it invariably draws laughs, for the surprise effect, which always pisses you off). Also, Sam needs to loosen up when a crowd's too subdued. Instead of relaxing and not caring, he tenses up, works harder to win the room over, but then starts floundering, everyone senses he's trying too hard, and it's painful to watch. Whenever that happens, you feel great. Whenever you're better than Sam, you feel great. Being better than Sam is what you've wanted since your first day at the National Comedy School. You thought that at least after you graduated, you wouldn't always be competing with him, but the joke's on you. By being around each other so much, you've become friends, and you work well together, so you collaborate on projects, and you're often booked together for comedy nights. No doubt about it, you guys are joined at the hip. Sam's charming. People like him right off the bat.

Sam had an earbud in, his iPhone in one hand, open on the Dictaphone playing his set from tonight, his eyes staring into space, his lips mouthing the words to each gag, his eyebrows scrunching up when he wasn't satisfied with his performance or the crowd's reaction.

You felt no need to listen to your set right away. You knew you'd done better than Sam. That was all that mattered.

But things have worked out for Sam, you have to give him that. There's a reason Forand signed him and started managing his career, even before you guys graduated.

But, though you like Sam, you secretly disdain him too. You can't help it. It's almost impossible not to have some contempt for the work of a comic you've knocked around with for two years at school and a few years on the scene. Comedy requires an element of mystery, of the unknown, but with Sam, you know every nook and cranny of his soul even better than he does. You know what makes him tick, turns him on, makes him cry. There isn't any part of him that can surprise you now. Even his new jokes sound to you like you've heard them a hundred times before.

Still, you like him. You like the guy. It's just kinda complicated because, like you, he wants everybody to like him, so you're always competing. And it's kinda complicated because deep down you envy him. You wish Forand had signed *you*. Forand not signing you is Forand telling you you're crap, Forand telling you you're worthless, Forand telling you you're unlikable.

Your phone vibrated in your pocket. It was that girl again.

9

The one you'd slept with a dozen times and hadn't seen in two months.

"Whatcha up to?" she said in the voice of a five-year-old.

"Wanna come over?" she went on, slurring a bit because after seven p.m., she liked her wine.

"Um, I...what? No, I can't."

Sam's hand moved up to his earbud, pulled it out.

The girl started pleading: "*Pleeeeease* come over. I need to see you."

"You need to see me? But we...I mean we haven't seen each other in like a really long time."

"Exactly! I never hear from you."

"I, um, yeah...no."

"No?"

"I'm not coming over. I don't feel like it."

"Oh, come on!"

"Why?"

"I really wanna see you."

"Your timing's not great."

"Oh, come *ooooon!*"

"I'm serious."

"I've already opened a bottle of wine. I can't drink the whole thing myself."

A lie: she could easily down that bottle—and probably a second one too.

"No, I can't make it."

"I'll pay your taxi."

"I'm not at home. It's just not a good time. I'm on my way to a party."

"Can I come?"

"No."

"After then? Come over after your party, and I'll be waiting in bed naked."

You saw a flicker of interest in Sam's eyes. Not sexual interest, more like morbid curiosity, rubbernecking to see a car accident in the other lane on a highway. You realized you should've put in your earphones because even though you weren't on speaker, Sam could hear everything.

"I'm gonna hang up now, okay?"

Something like a sob on the other end of the line. Then a deep breath.

"You're a MOTHERFUCKING ASSHOLE!"

"Alright, okay. Good night."

You had no time to recoup before the messages started flooding in on Messenger:

Really you treat me so shitty

Just fuck off

You need to get over yourself

ok

ok

ok

ok

Raph it's all good, I'm calming down

But just come by

Come

Come over ok

Please

Alright?

It'll be fun

That girl could type fast. It was all over in three minutes. Normally, that meant you'd have some peace for at least a month, till her next meltdown. It was fun at times to turn up at her place at three a.m., polish off a few bottles of wine, and screw till morning, but it'd become less fun once you realized she'd toss back the wine every night of the week and should never be trusted with a cellphone while under the influence. No matter—we all have our strengths and our weaknesses. She can't hold her liquor, and you don't have the guts to block her.

"You okay, bro?"

Sam had watched you deal with the situation without saying a word. Now he cocked an eyebrow, held back a smirk. You know Sam. You can decipher every little inflection in his voice, read every subtle variation in his expression.

Sam relished his question. By saying, "You okay, bro?" he was telling you he thought, as usual, that you were sleeping with a total bitch, that you'd gotten tangled up in some ridiculous drama, probably to get attention. By asking if everything was alright, he was questioning your ability to interact with other human beings. He was making you look like an irresponsible teenager. He was dumping on you.

You felt you should explain yourself. "I swear I hadn't spoken to her in two months. She's crazy."

"Mm."

"It's the same old story every time."

"Get your shit together, dude. It's not normal."

It would've been worse to defend yourself, so you just hunched over and made do with a shrug. Sometimes, you wished you knew Sam just a little less. There's a point beyond which we know people too well to really appreciate them.

To change the subject, you said, "Is Forand's assistant gonna be there?"

You'd spoken in a tone that suggested you were joking, to hide the fact that you weren't at all. You're not the king of subterfuge.

You'd pretended you'd forgotten my name.

You thought you were being so smooth, reducing me to my job title: assistant to his manager. You didn't want it to be obvious you'd set your sights on me.

I hadn't been a fantasy of yours, not really, but Sam had seen you look at me too long one night after a gig, when I was sitting with you guys and Forand, and before you even wondered anything about me, Sam said, "She's single, y'know." That threw you for a loop. You know your place in the world, and you know that guys like you don't end up with girls like me. But Sam had set a trap, and so you started thinking of me as a possibility.

You figured I probably wouldn't remember you anyway. You were still too "junior." The night we all shared a table at Le Bordel, you weren't even on the bill. At one point, you tried lightening the mood so it'd seem a little less ridiculous that you had to count your change to pay for your beer. I ended up paying for you, not out of pity but because you were wasting my precious time. It was less annoying to treat you to a pint than sit there while you counted your dimes and tried making me laugh. By the next day, I'd forgotten all about you.

I work for a talent agency, so I'm used to young comedians trying to make me laugh to cover up their shortcomings. It takes more to impress me. You weren't even unpleasant enough to leave a lasting impression. But that was a good thing because I still had an open mind about you.

And you wanted to make a good impression. Ever since Sam told you I was single, you'd been stalking me. You hadn't managed to find out much because I'm one of those people who've learned they have more to gain by lying low than by standing out. But you found out what you needed: that I'm as pretty in pictures as I am in a dimly lit comedy club.

Information is governed by supply and demand. If we give

less, it's worth more. Show just a bit of skin, and a naked ankle is enough to trigger whole nights of erotic dreams.

So in an exaggeratingly casual and detached tone, you said, "Is Forand's assistant gonna be there?"

If I was there, you figured you could go up to me, make some comment about my trip to Iceland—because that was one of the only things you'd found out about me, that I'd gone to Iceland last year—and you then could maybe start forming a more complete picture of me.

"Uh, yeah, I did invite her actually. Why?"

You'd asked as a joke. You didn't expect me to really be there. But knowing I would be, you suddenly became flustered. You didn't know why you were going to the party or why you'd asked that question or what your intentions were toward me. Or what Sam thought of your interest in me.

Sam was probably not a rival since I work for his manager. He doesn't have many principles, but he knows it's not good for business to fuck the payroll. But Sam doesn't necessarily want what's best for you. Telling him you fantasize about seeing the ankles of his manager's hot assistant would be exposing yourself too much and giving him your heart to cruelly rip to shreds. Being mean is good for a laugh, and getting a laugh is all you guys know how to do.

You shifted in your seat and tried to appear nonchalant. "Oh, I dunno," you said. "Just wondering."

It was a long shot whether I'd be at the party. I had no reason to be there, but I had nothing to do tonight, and Sam invited me almost as a joke, when I'd called earlier to work out the details for a corporate event he'd be doing in Mont-Laurier in two weeks.

You pressed ahead: "So what's she up to?"

"Laurie?"

"Yeah."

Sam didn't understand your question. "Well, she's coming to the party," he said.

"No, I mean what does she do?"

"Well, uh, she's Forand's assistant."

"She must do other things."

"I think she told me she writes."

"Oh yeah?"

"She wants to be a comedy writer, I think. Or anyway, she's trying, she's starting out."

"She any good?"

"I've never seen anything. But she's smart, so it must be good."

Sam lifted his eyes from his phone, looked into yours. "She's cool, Laurie. Very cool."

It wasn't weird, how he said that. It was more like a truce, or an apology. *She's cool, so it's good you're interested in her, I think it's great, I'd warn you if there were any red flags.* He would've said that out loud if you guys could talk other than through jokes.

The taxi slowed down in front of the apartment building. Sam took out his credit card. "I'll get it, Raph," he said.

"No, no, it's fine."

"Okay, I'll give you a beer upstairs."

You had forty dollars left in your account. By forking out twenty for the ride (your credit was maxed out, of course), you knew you'd need to find a way to survive on your remaining twenty till you got paid for tonight's gig. It wasn't so bad. You'd rather go hungry a few days than let Sam pay and rub it in that he made way more money than you.

As you went up the stairs, a thrill slid down your throat, ran down your spine, then warmed your belly. Jitters, maybe.

You felt good when you grasped the doorknob to the apartment. The best part of any party is the moment just before you open the door.

THE HUMIDITY, THE CIGARETTES, THE STINK OF THE DUDE near the entranceway, who thought nobody would notice he'd let one rip, the spilled beer drying sticky in a corner that the party's host will curse tomorrow, the sweat, the bad breath, the beer burps—a bouquet of the most disgusting and comforting smells in the world greeted you when you walked through the front door.

Sam leaned into you. "Game on, man," he whispered.

You stood straighter and scanned the length of the apartment to take an inventory of everyone there.

Max Lap was leaning against a wall in the hallway. "Raph Massi! Brrrap!" he cried, then came over to give you a smacking high-five and a bear hug. "You good, bro?"

"Yeah, I'm alright. But you, you'd better cut back on the chicken." You patted his belly, which had gotten bigger in the past few months.

"Occupational hazard," he said with a laugh.

Max had done pretty well since the comedy school, and his career got a major unexpected boost when he began sampling all the fried chicken sold at restaurants across Montreal and making YouTube videos out of his experience. The videos had gone viral, so restaurants started offering him dinner on the house, first in Montreal, then all across Quebec. The scheme had paid off so well that his stand-up had practically become a sideline, even though he insisted he was a comedian first and a YouTuber second, not the other way around. If he was Sam, you'd take every opportunity to exploit his inferiority complex, but this was Max Lap, and you weren't close enough to the guy to be that snarky.

Pointing to your case of beer, you said, "I'm gonna park this in the fridge, then we should catch up." You patted his shoulder. "I wanna talk."

That wasn't actually true. You liked trading one-liners with Max whenever you ran into him, you really did like him, he was a pretty nice guy back in school, but speaking to him too long made you a little anxious because you didn't have much to say when you two were talking face to face. It was no big deal, but it'd be embarrassing for you both if you admitted that to him. For you, what mattered most was that you appeared to want to get deep, but not that you actually did it. You were all about appearances.

As you cut through the living room, you saw Dom Montigny from behind, engrossed in a game of beer pong. To surprise him, you pinched his love handles and yelled, "Heads up!"

Dom yelped and everyone in the room turned. He'd automatically thrown his ball, which landed in his opponent's last red Solo cup. The other guy, for some reason, was shirtless.

"Dude, you can't do that while I'm laser-focused," Dom said.

"You should thank me. I just won you the game."

You pointed to Mr. Pecs, who was downing the beer that the ball had landed in.

"Okay, okay," Dom said. "Here, take a beer. I have too many."

He gave you one of his cups of beer, then gave your butt a slap as you headed farther into the apartment. Going by the dining room, you spotted Elena Miller leaning against a china cabinet and staring at her phone. You gave her a kiss on the cheek. "Ms. Miller," you said.

"Mr. Massicotte."

"Loved that bit you did about the Winter Carnival at ComediHa."

"Wow, that's the first compliment you've given me since we graduated."

"If I'm too nice to you, you might get the wrong idea."

"What kind of idea? You're scared I might think you've finally learned how to function in society?"

"Y'know, you could just say thanks."

She looked up from her phone, gave you a genuine smile.

"Thanks, Raph. That was sweet of you."

"I mean it. Really, you were solid. It's a miracle that after putting up with you for two years at school, I still like what you do."

"It's called talent, kid." Elena glanced toward Mr. Pecs. "Now, be on your best behaviour, okay?" she whispered. "I'm here with my new boyfriend."

"One way to get me to misbehave is to tell me to behave."

She tried looking peeved but couldn't wipe the smirk off her face.

"How long before you cheat on him?" you asked.

"Asshole."

"Because I'm worried about you. I know monogamy's not your forte. You must be miserable."

"So you'll be kind enough to invite me to your place to save me, right?"

"Normally, I would, since I've got a big heart, but I've got my sights set elsewhere tonight."

"I'll believe that when I see it."

"Your boyfriend lose his shirt? I have an old T-shirt in my bag."

"Raph, we both know that if you had the discipline and genetics to have a gorgeous chest like his, you'd walk around shirtless all day long."

"True. That's why I have a belly, to spare you all."

An arm appeared out of nowhere to grab Elena's beer. Mr. Pecs had slid between you and her to steal a gulp of her beer. Sweat beaded on his chest. There was a sudden muskox smell in the air.

"I'm Jason." He said it like he didn't really expect a response. Instead of extending a hand to shake, he chugged Elena's beer without taking his eyes off you.

You stared at him awhile, then said, "I just set up a GoFundMe page to buy you a T-shirt. By the end of the night, we should have enough money to cover your tits. I told Elena it was mean of her not to pitch in to buy you some clothes, but she insists she shouldn't have to foot the bill."

"Huh?"

"Your career's going great," you said to Elena. "So the least you could do is help your boyfriend out."

The dude acted like he couldn't understand the language you were speaking. Elena looked uncomfortable, but also ready to crack up. "André said to put the beer in the bathtub, Raph," she muttered, nodding toward the bathroom.

You walked away with a grin on your face. As you went into the bathroom, André was coming out, sniffing and rubbing his gums, and you collided, knocking heads.

You took a step back. "Oh shit, man! I'm sorry!"

"No, no, it was my fault!" André took a half second to recognize you. "Oh, Raph!"

"Hey, bro!"

"You okay?"

In the heat of the moment, you pretended you'd lost the

ability to speak. "I...can't...form...words."

André stood there frozen, butt clenched, wondering if he'd have to live with the guilt of cutting short a comedian's career. One golden moment. You left him dangling a good five seconds, then yelled, "You're so fucking gullible!"

André pretended to punch you in the face, then had a good laugh. "Dude, you're such a dick," he said. "Where you coming from?"

"Jockey."

"You breaking in your one-man show?"

A little cloud of shame hovered over your head. "No, no, well technically yes, eventually," you said, "but I don't have a contract yet for a one-man show. It's Sam who—"

"Right, right, it's Sam who signed with Forand and is putting a show together. Fuck, that guy's on a roll, right?"

Sam had hundreds of thousands of views on YouTube with his sketches. He was always on TV and radio. Even people out in the sticks knew who Sam was. You, not so much.

"André?"

"Yeah?"

You rubbed your nose as a sign to him.

He quickly rubbed his nostrils, feigning embarrassment. "Oops," he said with an almost complicit look. He patted you on the back, then walked off.

You went into the bathroom. There was a filthy tub filled with ice and already overflowing with beer, so you gave up on that idea and headed out onto the balcony instead. It's mild out tonight, maybe seven or eight degrees, which seemed fine for beer. Once the beer hit room temperature, you'd probably be too hammered to notice anyway.

Because, yeah, you had to get pretty drunk to drum up the courage to come talk to me. Speaking onstage to two hundred people was a breeze, but trying to get a laugh out of a girl who you'd only spoken to once and had your eye on, now that took guts.

"Who else is coming tonight?" Sam had come up behind you on the balcony, making you jump. He put his two six-packs of Pabst down beside your case of Tremblay, then opened a pack of Bensons, stuck a cigarette in his mouth, and handed you a smoke, even though you hadn't asked for one.

Sam smoked Bensons. Of course he smoked Bensons. Not for the quality. Just so people would see he smoked Bensons, whereas you smoked Craven A.

He cupped a hand around his lit lighter, brought it toward your mouth. You took a long drag. Your mind cleared, your shoulders loosened. Life was good.

We spend our whole lives running around in search of happiness, when all we need to be happy is a long drag on a smoke when the time's right for a long drag on a smoke.

"I dunno if the floor will hold any more people," you said.

"Thomas said he'd come too, I think," Sam said.

"Of course he'll come."

"If he's coming to the party, he could've come to your gig."

Another sly put-down. Sam's manager followed him practically everywhere, and what Sam was likely implying was that you weren't being well managed by Thomas. Sam was probably right. Thomas had been in your year at school, and about two months after graduating, he realized he'd never make it as a comedian. He decided on a whim to become a manager, and since you two got along fine and no one else was itching to sign you, he figured you guys could team up. It wasn't a match made in heaven, like Forand and Sam, but it would do. Maybe Thomas wasn't the best manager ever, but there was no denying he made a better manager than a comedian.

He'd been in the biz only two years, so he was still learning the ropes. He didn't have any big names on his roster yet. You and Sam smoked in silence, staring down at the alleyway. It was bathed in orangey light from a street lamp. A cat in heat was howling like a banshee and rubbing against a wooden fence. Below you, a couple of boomers, tipsy on wine, were finishing their supper.

"Your set killed tonight," Sam said. "Totally killed."

"Thanks. I think I could come up with a better closer, but one thing at a time, I guess."

"Well, we can always come up with a better closer, but sooner or later, we gotta let go."

"Yeah."

He didn't add anything more—no bitchiness, no thorn on that rose he'd just handed you.

"Me and you should do a double bill at Zoofest next summer. Like a half-hour each. I'll have stuff to test out for my one-man show. And it might be the kick in the ass you need to write more material. It could help you find a producer for your own show."

Okay, so now you had your thorn. Sam's subtext was this: "You're slow, you aren't productive, you aren't disciplined, I've pulled ahead of you since we left school." And yet he was totally right. You're a good stand-up, that's not the issue. But you also love to loaf around, smoke weed, play *Call of Duty*—things that aren't exactly career boosters.

"I'm down," you said. "If they want a no-name on the bill."

"Forand can get us in."

"Your manager works for you, not me."

"We'll see about that."

You flicked your cigarette butt off the balcony. It landed

directly in the wineglass of the downstairs neighbour. He looked up, yelled, "Hey, my yard's not a fucking ashtray!"

You and Sam started laughing. Sam yelled back, "If I was you, I'd hang on to that butt. It'll be worth a mint in a couple years."

You both turned around to watch the party through the kitchen window. "Is Laurie coming or not?" you asked.

"She's here." Sam pointed me out in the kitchen. You thought I looked even prettier than you'd remembered. There was something in my face that drew you to me, like how we're drawn to a fire in the winter. Something comforting.

Even though it was only the second time you'd seen me, you felt like it was a reunion of sorts, seeing me there in the kitchen. Once we hook up, you'll often say, "I wish I'd always known you." But me knowing the younger you would've been terrible. You'd probably be scared that if I'd known you back in high school, I would've despised you just like everybody else did. We wouldn't have been in the same league. Everyone liked me in high school. I've always been good with people, even when I was younger. As for you, you had to learn. The hard way.

In the kitchen, on the other side of the door, I was chatting to a girl you didn't know, one hand resting on her shoulder, our faces close together. The girl had baby bangs and intricate sleeve tattoos.

"Is she into women?" you asked Sam.

"Nah, I don't think so."

"You know that for a fact?"

"Chill, man. You won't die if she's a lesbian."

You forced a laugh to lighten the mood. No, of course, you wouldn't die. Because, statistically, there was a much greater chance that I wouldn't be into you. You had to accept that, or else you'd be a psychopath.

"Okay, I'm gonna go talk to her," you said.

"Right now?"

"Bad timing?"

"I was just hoping you'd hang with me a half-hour before I lost you for the night."

Your legs tensed up. One wanted to move forward, the other wanted to stay back.

"Just kidding, man," Sam said, almost benevolently. "Go talk to her."

"Okay."

"Just don't be weird with her, okay?"

"I can't make any promises."

You downed your beer, handed the can to Sam, took a deep breath, opened the balcony door. You slipped into the musky-smelling kitchen and waited patiently, like a hunter, for Claire (the girl I was talking to) to wander off. Once she was gone, you came over and stood right in front of me. "Hey, I just found out you're not a lesbian, and I'm real happy about that," you said. "Wanna do shots?"

I didn't burst out laughing like you'd hoped, but I did crack a smile. You were very in-my-face, which was the only way you knew how to be.

"Why'd you think I was queer?"

"Just how you were talking to that girl a minute ago."

"Claire?" I turned to point to her. She was dancing in the living room, arms in the air, eyes closed, sweat beading on the tip of her nose.

"Yeah, her."

"She's my best friend," I said. "She just got back today from a four-month trip. I love her, but not in that way."

"Excellent news."

"Yeah, for who?" I said with a grin. "So what do you wanna drink?"

"Actually, I've just got beer. Doing shots was just my opening line."

"Don't make promises you can't keep."

You couldn't help smiling. I hadn't slammed the door in your face, and that was already a big victory.

"Wanna do vodka pickles?" you said.

"Sounds like the worst shot ever."

"But you've never tried it."

"No."

"So you can't say it's the worst ever."

Something about your insistence seemed to amuse me. I wasn't won over by you, but you could see I was at least curious.

"True," I grudgingly admitted, still grinning.

"So we've got ourselves a project."

You rummaged through the kitchen cabinets looking for shot glasses, but all you found were small water glasses. You grabbed two of them.

"Well, it won't be as impressive as it would be in a bar, but it's the effort that counts, right?"

"I bet they haven't got pickles either."

"Everyone has pickles."

"Not sure they'd like you searching through—"

But you were already kneeling in front of the open fridge, moving aside cans of Coke, wilted vegetables, Tupperware filled with mouldy leftovers. Your eyes fell on a jar of jumbo pickles, which you then held up like a trophy.

"Those are sweet pickles," I said. "I'm pretty sure you use dill pickles in drinks. And they're too freaking big for shots."

You stuck your hand in the jar, pulled out a pickle at least six inches long. Broke off two pieces, dropped one into each glass.

"I hope you washed your hands," I said.

"Yeah, I'm super OCD about that."

"I can't decide if I find this funny or just gross."

"They'll be soaking in alcohol, so there's no risk of germs."

You scanned the kitchen counter, but the only vodka you saw was an empty bottle of Smirnoff, so you settled for a litre of Beefeater gin instead.

"Whose is that?" I asked.

"No idea."

You took a swig from the bottle while looking me in the eye. Then poured a few ounces over each chunk of pickle.

"Officially the worst shot anyone's ever made me in my life," I said.

"As long as it's memorable, I'll be happy."

I lifted my glass. You clinked yours against mine.

"I'm Laurie, by the way."

"I know. We've already met."

"I know."

"But you don't remember. Or do you?"

"Technically, no. But I do know you're gonna tell me we met at Le Bordel."

You pause, then say, "How'd you know?"

"Because I have a superpower."

"Oh, really?"

"I can see into the future."

"How?"

"We barely know each other. I'm not gonna reveal all my secrets. But I *can* tell you I'm clairvoyant."

"So what does the future hold for me?"

"You can't handle it."

You smile, hold back a little chuckle. "Okay, prove it," you say.

I take a breath, glance toward the balcony. For a fraction of a second, you sense I've become extremely, irreparably, infinitely sad. But then I swallow my sadness, smile again, look directly at you. "You told yourself nothing bad could happen," I say.

"I...what?"

Your diaphragm stops working momentarily, and your knees go weak. The music from the living room drops twenty decibels. You're suddenly looking at me through a tunnel.

Because, yes, you did tell yourself back in the taxi that nothing bad could happen tonight. After a pause, you frown and say, "But you said you could see into the future."

"Uh-huh."

"But that's my past."

"I know about it since you're gonna tell me about it later."

"Well, if you take that angle, everything can seem to come from the future."

"Okay. There's a crazy girl you sleep with who called you in the cab."

"Did Sam tell you that?"

"Nope, I haven't spoken to Sam since you guys got here."

"Does sleeping with a crazy chick reflect badly on me?"

"Calling her crazy reflects badly on you."

"You started it."

"You called her crazy in the cab."

"So what's gonna happen, if you're not bullshitting me?"

LET'S START WITH THE MOST IMPORTANT THING: THE SEX tonight will be really good. Even though we'll go home plastered. I won't cum, but you won't realize it, and I won't tell you right away, obviously, so I don't hurt your feelings. I know how fragile a guy's ego can be. But it'll still be good sex. I'm not going into details because I don't want to spoil the surprise. But really good sex, I guarantee it.

We have a connection, you and me. It's obvious. And even if sex isn't everything, for two people who meet to take the same path together, they need a bond. And for the lack of anything better, sex often does the job of holding people together. We like to keep love and sex totally separate to justify all the times we fuck and nothing happens. But this strategy can fail us, even if it happens just once in a lifetime. Someone turns a corner and suddenly meets a stranger in the right place at the right time. They come together and drive each other crazy because of things as trivial as the smell of their sweat, the texture of their skin, the shape of their mouths, the tone of their voices. Desire is just a lure. But who cares if it's a lure as long as the fish bites.

That's why tomorrow morning, as soon as you step out of my apartment, you'll realize you're in deep trouble. You'll have a hangover and be late for a brainstorming session for some lame web series you plan to develop with some inept producer (it'll never get off the ground, I assure you).

You won't even remember where you are exactly, or how to get back home, and yet it'll hit you like a baseball bat to the face—between now and tomorrow, something pretty major will happen to alter the trajectory of your life.

As of tomorrow morning, seeing me will be all that counts. As of tomorrow morning, you'll be unhinged.

You won't know why or how it happened. It's not like you to get attached to just any girl who comes along. You're not that desperate.

But there's a time and place for everything, and maybe tomorrow morning, outside my apartment door, your eyes squinting from the sun, your mouth dry as chalk, and your soul pretty much dead, it might be the perfect time and place for you to fall in love.

From then on, you'll know full well you can't play games, pretend, string me along. Because you'll know that girls like me—if you piss them off—they're out of your life.

From then on, you'll start to stress out, fear you'll lose me. From then on, you'll know something bad might've really happened tonight.

I THINK YOU'RE BEAUTIFUL. THIS IS AN IMPORTANT DETAIL in our story.

I tell you so. I'll whisper it in your ear later, tonight, while we're fucking, while you're bent over me and I'm clutching you, my eyes staring into yours, my hands around your neck, my calves tight around your back: "You're beautiful." I'll say it again, later. It'll always be true. But you'll never really believe me, not tonight, not ever, not completely. Which is understandable because until cégep, you often got called fat and ugly. So it's normal that you think I'm bullshitting when I say you're beautiful.

This never stopped you from scoring. You could still get girls. You realized pretty quick in high school that improv troupes exist so less attractive people can fuck too.

You're not monstrous or repulsive. You don't have any obvious deformities or even irregular features. You're not obese (just a bit of a beer belly, nothing major). You're not too tall or too short. In a crowd, you wouldn't stand out. You look like a stock photo. You're *normal*. A six out of ten.

But in high school, it was maybe just a misalignment of the stars that painted a target on your back—your braces, your poor fashion choices, a comment you let slip at the wrong time—and for five years, everybody decided you were the resident freak.

You're not the kind of guy who easily forgets, so you still feel real hatred for those kids who trashed you all through high school. Worse—you still believe what they said.

That's why you won't quite believe me when I say you're beautiful. Some shadowy part of you will believe I'm stroking your cheek just so you'll be even more startled when I up and slap you.

As for the kids who called you fat and ugly in high school, you felt you'd stuck it to them when you went out on the improv stage and got them laughing so hard they cried. Because then, at least, you got to choose when and on what terms they could laugh at you. You owe your career to the fact that you don't like yourself.

Given all that, you won't want to go out in public with me for at least a month. You'll want to wait to make sure I don't see you as a pity fuck, or maybe I'm waiting for my order of contact lenses to come in and can't see what you really look like yet.

You'll take me to a comedy night at Le Terminal, where you plan to test out a new bit. The doorman downstairs will stop you before you can head up. "Sorry, man," he'll say. "The club's not open yet."

"But...I'm on the bill tonight," you'll say.

"You're in the show?"

"I'm totally in the show."

"But I don't recognize you."

"You know every stand-up in town?"

"Well, I do work here, so yeah."

"I've done a couple sets here."

"Well, they must not have been that memorable."

I'll go up to the doorman, give him my angelic smile. "He's with me," I'll say.

The doorman's face will light up. "Hey there, Laurie! Yeah, okay. Go on in."

You'll go quiet on the way up. I'll put a hand on your

shoulder. "You realize that was just a cockfight, right?" I'll say.

"I'm lousy at cockfights."

"Well, it seemed to go okay tonight."

"Thanks to you."

"That a problem?" That'll get a smile out of you.

Max Lap and Sam will see you come upstairs with me. They'll join us at the bar while we're ordering. Sam will lean against the counter, arms crossed, and stare at us with a cocky smile. "You two still hooking up?" he'll say.

I'll smirk and say, "Want me to send you a record of all my past conquests too?"

"You know my email," he'll say. "I want it in my inbox by nine a.m. tomorrow." Sam will turn toward the tables, which are gradually filling up with people. "Don't expect to be bowled over tonight," he'll add. "I'm not doing any new material."

"Oh, I'm not here to see you, darling," I'll say. "Tonight's not a work night for me."

"Sorry, bro," you'll say. "The earth doesn't revolve *just* around you."

Max Lap, who looks gigantic behind Sam, will pass a pint over Sam's shoulder and place it in his hand. "Now you guys leave poor Sammy alone," he'll say. "You know he's a sensitive boy."

Max Lap will raise his glass, and we'll all clink glasses, then take big gulps.

"I'm gonna head to the green room," you'll tell me.

I'll grip your arm before you leave. Draw you to me, plant a kiss on your lips. You'll immediately glance around like you've just committed some immoral act—kissing a girl in public who you consider ten times better-looking than you.

"Break a leg," I'll say with a smile.

33

"Will do." You'll smile back at me. "Sit wherever you want, or just stand at the back if you like. I'll see you after my set—"

"Raph, I come to shows like this three times a week. I don't need a guided tour of the place."

You'll let out a laugh. "Yeah, that's true. Alright, see you."

You and the guys will all go to the green room, which smells like a hockey bag. Sam will recap a Joe Rogan podcast he played for Max while Max reviews his set on his phone. André will host that night, replacing the usual emcee, who's been mysteriously "missing" for a month (Thomas has already let slip that the dude was hospitalized for a few weeks after a manic episode during which he made an offer on a house in Arizona).

Thomas will come into the green room and stay standing since there are no chairs left. "Yo, Raph, I brought you a beer," he'll say, handing it over.

First you'll guzzle the half-pint you have left, then quickly start on the second beer.

Thomas will give you a suspicious look. "Raph, stand up," he'll say.

You won't understand, but you'll comply.

"Turn around."

"What?"

"Turn, Raph. I wanna see you from the back."

You'll glance at the others and roll your eyes. "It starts off all professional," you'll say, "then next thing you know, your manager's checking out your ass."

"What's up with you, Raph?" Thomas will say.

"What?"

"I go on holiday three weeks and you change shape."

"Raph's discovered sex," Sam will say. "So he's melting away before our very eyes."

"No, no," you'll groan. "I'm just eating a bit better and toking up less nowadays."

"Because of a girl," Sam will add.

"It's great you're taking care of yourself. But just don't turn into a fitness buff and end up looking like Robert Pattinson, okay? Handsome dudes aren't funny. The people coming to see you guys tonight don't wanna be turned on by you. They want you to be their loud brother-in-law who's a hoot at family parties. Look at Jonah Hill. Now that he's slimmed down, nobody thinks he's funny."

"Thom, I've lost five pounds."

"They want you to be their wacky brother-in-law for one night, then never think about you again. You gotta be good in small doses, not inhabit their fantasies. And who's this girl you've lost five pounds for?"

"Michel Forand's assistant," Sam will say.

"Oh, so he's sleeping with the enemy," Thomas will whine. You'll sigh and say, "Thom, get over it."

"You won't get Forand to sign you by sleeping with his assistant," Thomas will say. "You know that, right?"

Sam will bark a laugh, throw a crumpled ball of paper at you. "No worries," he'll say. "Forand isn't gonna sign Raph."

"Thanks for your support, boys," you'll say, rolling your eyes.

Two light taps on the door, then the stage manager will slip into the room. "Five minutes to showtime," she'll say. "Ready, guys?"

André, who's spent the last little while bent over his notebook, will finally look up. "Sam, I'll plug your previews that start in January," he'll say. "Anything else to promote?"

"I've got my radio features on Rouge FM, my TikTok, my Instagram. And my pieces on the Sports Network."

"Great. Max, your YouTube channel, but no upcoming show?"

"Nope."

"Raph?"

"Um, Instagram, I guess."

Sam will stifle a laugh, then snort. "Raph, your Instagram is like three or four pictures of food, plus stories of you losing it when you get stuck in traffic."

André won't put Sam in his place, but he'll at least give you a sympathetic smile.

"Nothing to plug, André. Thanks," you'll say.

"Okay, so remember the lineup tonight is Raph, Max, then Sam," André will say. "After intermission, Elena Miller and Philippe-Audrey are up. They here yet?"

"I haven't seen them," the stage manager will say.

"Oh, great. Have fun, boys!"

André will follow the stage manager out.

Before Thomas leaves, he'll say to you, "You is smart, you is kind, you is important."

Max Lap will take a gulp of his beer. There'll be an awkward pause, then he'll say, "So things serious with Laurie?"

"I dunno, bro. It's been like a month."

"But is it heading in that direction?"

"If Sam stops sabotaging me, maybe..."

Pint in hand, Sam will give you a bear hug from behind. "Oh, come on, big boy," he'll say. "You know I'm happy for you." He'll accidentally tilt his beer, spill half of it down your front.

"Dude, you're such a dumb-ass!" you'll cry. "Anyone got an extra T-shirt?"

"Sorry, bro," Max Lap will say. "I've got fuck all."

You'll hear the house applauding. André will start his

crowd work on the other side of the green-room wall.

"Knowing André, you've got a good half-hour for your T-shirt to dry," Max will say. "His intro's always way too long."

"Alright," you'll say. "See you guys." Your hand on the doorknob, you'll add, "Don't take it personal, Sam, but I might come vomit onstage during your set."

Sam will blow you a kiss, give you the finger.

I'll catch your eye as soon as you leave the green room. While you watch André warm up the crowd, you'll chug the beer Thomas gave you. You'll achieve a kind of peace as you finish your pint. If you don't get two beers in you, you can't go onstage without your heart crawling out of your mouth, even just for a tight five at Le Terminal.

André's warm-up will be going good till he riles up some butch with a round of jokes on female truckers. Your pulse will slowly speed up as the minutes pass. As per usual, but as per usual is still hard on the heart. When André passes the twenty-minute mark, you'll know you're on soon and force yourself to slow down your breathing.

"He got out of the comedy school almost two years ago, and the best I can say about the dude is he's very punctual. Too bad he's barely functional. Give it up for Raph Massi!"

The crowd will applaud. I'll turn and give you a wink. You'll walk through the audience, give André a high-five as you pass him on the stairs. When you get to centre stage, you'll catch Thomas's eye. He's frowning, and you'll remember your T-shirt is half-soaked with beer and you can't just pretend everything's normal.

"Hey there, guys, sorry about my shirt," you'll say. "I'm lactating at the moment, and it's a real bitch."

A polite laugh from the room.

"If any of you can suggest a milk pump for men, lemme know."

The laugh will grow a bit louder.

"And if anyone wants to go breastfeed my baby in the dressing room, that'd be sweet. I'm kinda afraid it might start bawling during my set, which would be super awkward."

You'll look out at me. "I brought a date to the show tonight. Don't tell her I've got a kid."

That'll get a smile out of me. All of a sudden, you'll feel your backbone straighten and a warmth spread through your gut. You'll figure you've explained your wet T-shirt enough and can now pivot to your set. Things will go pretty good, except for one thing: you'll have a tough time looking away from me. Because you'll know that if you aren't good-looking enough for me, you at least have to be funny enough.

The crowd will laugh. They'll laugh a lot. But you'll barely even notice because you're performing your set in a twilight zone, a parallel world where I'm the only person sitting in the audience.

As soon as we step outside at intermission (neither of us will want to stay for the second half since we're in a rush to go home and fuck), you'll say, "No stress if you didn't like my set."

"Okay, but if I say I liked it, will you believe me?"

"Dunno. Try it."

I'll take a breath, look you in the eye. "I loved it." I'll step forward, stand on tippytoe, give you a gentle kiss on the lips.

"Remember what they say about seeing people onstage," you'll say.

"What?"

"Never crush on someone you see onstage. If you do, you'll be sorry when you get to know them in real life."

"Look, my first impression of you was those sorry-ass vodka pickles you made, so things can only get better."

Far behind me, you'll spot Elena near the corner of the street. She'll be rushing along the sidewalk, almost running. When she reaches us, she'll be panting. "Has it started yet?" she'll say.

"No, no," you'll say. "It's still intermission."

"They screwed up the lineup at Le Jockey and put me on third. Fuck, I didn't think I'd make it here in time." She'll pause a second when she recognizes me, like she's solving some tricky brainteaser involving you and me. "Oh, Laurie," she'll say. "Hi!"

Then she'll throw you a smile—conspiratorial, almost impressed—before she heads toward the entrance. "Gotta fly!" Her hand on the door handle, she'll stop, turn. "Is Sam still up there?" she'll ask you.

"I think so. Why?"

She'll frown, look a bit concerned. "Oh, nothing. Have a good night, you guys."

She'll disappear into the club, leaving us floating in a bubble on Mount Royal Avenue. Light snow will be falling around us. Christmas lights will be sparkling. It'll be cool out, but not too cold. You'll drift out of your body, see yourself from far away standing beside me.

It'll hit you like a wave strong enough to knock you over. You've always dreamed of this moment. You've always dreamed of the day you'd meet the girl of your dreams who'd consider you the boy of her dreams. As a teenager, you'd picture yourself in a moment like this to relieve the pain and boredom of your life back then. At this very moment, your future and present will merge. You'll be at the right place at the right time. You'll feel a tingle inside, and it'll spur you on to say, "I love you, Laurie."

Something will shift in my eyes, contract a bit. But I won't say anything. Instead, I'll just kiss you.

A kiss won't be enough. You'll spend the rest of the night stewing, telling yourself you went too fast, lost your cool, startled me. I'll be no help. I'll act like nothing weird just happened. It's brutal, though, to tell someone you love them and hear nothing in return. It's earth-shattering.

That's the problem with being with me: you'll have to learn to navigate in the dark. After we split, you'll run into Claire one day and she'll say, "That's why we love Laurie so much. We always think she's being totally neutral, but she's got a lot hidden below the surface."

You'll want to scream at Claire that it's not cool to keep things hidden. The one time you'll dare to dig below the surface, I'll dump your ass.

I'LL END UP TELLING YOU I LOVE YOU, OBVIOUSLY I'LL END up telling you I love you, otherwise I wouldn't be spending the whole night telling you this story. I'll sound genuine when I say it, I'll look sincere, and I'll repeat it, say it often even. But the only way you'd believe without a doubt that I love you would be if the entire planet said it in unison with me. And that'll never happen, even if you work hard to make it happen.

Still, when I say it the first time, it'll have a huge effect on you. We'll be having sex for the third time that day. It'll be a Saturday and we'd spent three hours in bed earlier that morning, then forced ourselves to go out for brunch and get some sun, before we rushed back home because we couldn't find any better place to fuck.

As I'm cumming, I'll say, "I love you." Breathlessly, almost involuntarily.

Instead of feeling relief, you'll start crying. You'll lose your hard-on, pull out. You'll curl up in bed, your chest heaving violently.

"You okay?" I'll whisper, gently stroking your back.

You won't be able to speak. Because the only reply you could give would be absolutely pathetic.

If you could answer, you'd say you wished I loved you way more and way sooner. If I'd said "I love you" first, you wouldn't have started crying at all.

You aren't good with emotions. In your interactions with others, you're only good when more than three people are involved. Conversation's not your strong suit. How you communicate best is to put on a show.

So, from that point forward, that's what you'll fall back on.

WE'LL DO WHAT NORMAL COUPLES DO. NEXT SUMMER, everyone will go to Berlin, and to be like the cool kids, we'll go too. We'll book an amazing Airbnb in Kreuzberg. We'll rent fixies to bike around the whole city (we'll even do it twice). To get around town, we'll also spend three hundred euros on taxis, even though we can't afford it.

I'll let you take pictures of me, even let you put one or two on Instagram, so you can flaunt your trip but also show off your girlfriend, who you find so incredibly, perfectly, violently beautiful that when you look at her, it hurts, burns you up inside, tears you apart. There'll be one picture of me taken from behind as I lean on the edge of the Badeschiff swimming pool. I stare at the distant city and almost seem to be floating in the filthy water of the canal in front of us. There'll be a photo of me with a beer in a bar on the waterfront, my head tilted a little, my eyes a bit dull, so I don't look too posed. There'll be a photo of me watching karaoke in Mauerpark with hundreds of other people.

Because it's part of the experience, because we can't *not* do it, we'll line up to get into Berghain, even though it's not your scene. I won't need to twist your arm. You'll figure it's important to me because I mentioned the nightclub to you once, and as always, you'll do anything to please me.

We'll stand in line an hour and a half, so we have plenty of time to observe the protocol for getting in. The club will let in about one group out of two. You'll mentally prepare yourself not to moan all night if we're rejected. When we

43

finally reach the bouncer, he'll look at us awhile to prolong the suspense, probably because it's his job's only big perk, the power of life or death over the evening of a couple of poor Canadian tourists just minding their own business. Then, with a big grin, he'll jerk a thumb toward the entrance and say, "You're in."

We'll go up a few flights of stairs in a setting that perfectly captures what a tourist expects of an after-hours club in Berlin. A grungy space. Funky smells: pee, spilled beer, cigarettes, maybe the sour stench of vomit. High-contrast lighting with too many yellow and purple gels. A deep bass sound growing stronger as we climb the stairs.

Nights like this, you could have them in Montreal, but that's not the point. Anyway, you won't be there because you want to be. You aren't a big fan of clubs. They're for beautiful people who don't like to talk much—the opposite of you. You'll feel forced to feign interest and excitement only because *I* like this kind of nightlife, and if our interests differ too much, you'll figure I might up and leave you.

When we find the door leading to the main room, the music will roll over us like a tsunami. It'll be violent, it'll be *so* good, it'll be exactly what I need. Everything will become more complicated: moving, drinking, speaking. Clubbing and camping are much the same: they make life harder so we can get back to basics. You hate both equally.

I'll manage to find the way to the bar, slipping through a throng of sweaty bodies. We didn't drink anything beforehand, and I'll say I'm surprised how much easier it is to move around a club stone cold sober. I'll get us two beers. We'll find an opening on the crowded dance floor to shoehorn ourselves into.

You won't be having fun but can't bring yourself to tell

me. You'll figure you need a little something extra to handle being in such a big club. Over the music, you'll yell, "Wanna do drugs?"

I'll let out a laugh.

"I'm serious."

"Are you crazy? You crossed the border with drugs on you?"

"Of course not. But we could get something here, right?"

"You aren't scared we'll buy some bad shit and end up in the hospital?"

"First, I don't think it's more likely to happen here than in Montreal. Second, if it does happen, it'll make a damn good story. I can do a bit on it."

That'll make me smile. "I don't think your story's very relatable," I'll say.

"There's a way, I think, to make it funny."

"But first you gotta survive the night."

"Oh, I don't plan on dying. I'll just go a bit psycho."

"So what do we take?"

"We'll take what we can get. I'll be back, okay? I'm gonna go check out the bathroom. I'll meet you back here."

I'll raise my beer and smile. You'll head off but keep me in sight as long as you can before you turn away. Despite your disgust with sweaty bodies, you'll squeeze through the crowd to a more open area, then go up the first staircase you find. Naturally, you'll be too proud to ask where the bathroom is. You'll get lost in an almost pitch-dark maze. You'll come out at the entrance, then retrace your steps, find yourself back in the main room, then take another turn into a kind of lounge where you'll see bodies sprawled on beanbag chairs. Finally, you'll locate the unisex bathroom, two long rows of stalls stretching out endlessly on your left and right into the darkness.

You'll remember Sam saying you can always get drugs in a club bathroom. Sam's a good reference for these things. Unfortunately, he's never bothered telling you what to do once you're in the bathroom.

You'll lean against a wall and watch people go in and out of the stalls. A smiling redhead will enter a stall with another girl and, a minute and a half later, come back out and lean against the wall right next to you. You'll get all stressed out, but not because the situation's illegal or dangerous. No, what'll really worry you is how you look. You'll be scared you look like an idiot, or a predator, or a drug addict who suspects everyone else of being a drug addict. But you'll manage to quiet the little voice in your head that's always telling you that you're not worth shit. You'll muster the courage to say to the redhead, "Got anything to sell?"

She'll turn to you, smile, look friendly and professional, very customer service. She'll be like those sweet girls who work at Lush and massage your hand with a facial moisturizer while looking you in the eye and touting the virtues of jojoba oil or pineapple peels. The healthy, calm, well-balanced person you wish you were.

"Sure. Come with me."

You've never bought drugs from a stranger. This will be your first time. The girl won't exactly fit your image of a dealer. She'll have smooth skin, nice teeth, no circles under her eyes. She'll be straight out of a yogourt ad. She'll take you by the hand and lead you to a stall. The toilet has overflowed. The soles of your shoes will splash through a thin puddle of water on the floor.

"I'd like to buy, uh..."

As you speak, you'll picture the imaginary camera aimed at

you pulling back to show an aerial view of the club, then the neighbourhood, then Berlin, then Germany, then Europe, then planet Earth, till you shrink to a tiny dot. Your bright idea of buying drugs from a stranger in a foreign city will seem completely insane all of a sudden.

You can't finish your sentence, but the redhead will cut in: "I have MDMA."

"Uh, sure, I'll take two of those."

"They're ten euros each."

You'll have no idea how much molly should cost and you won't give a fuck. (If ever you remember our conversation tonight, one word of advice: if you pay more than seven euros a pill, you're getting screwed.) You'll open your wallet to find the right bill. Noticing you aren't too up on your euros, the redhead will point to a twenty-euro note.

She'll place two unsealed pills in your hand and thank you. You'll head off, practically run out of the bathroom. You'll find your way back to the dance floor, worried I've wandered off and that you'll spend the rest of the night looking for me while the two pills you hold tight in your hand melt away to nothing. But I'll still be there. I'll be standing—no, floating—in the crowd under a spotlight and smiling at you from a distance.

You'll make your way over to me. Open your hand and say, "Y'know, I've never taken this before."

"Me either," I'll say.

"So where the hell were we when everyone was doing it in high school?"

For you, the answer's easy. You were hiding at the back of the library. You weren't the kind of guy who got invited to parties.

Over the music, I'll yell, "I think girls who took molly

in high school are breastfeeding now, so it's a blessing in disguise."

You'll feel a little tickle at the back of your throat, a quiver up and down your spine, your head growing a little lighter—the excitement before you do something naughty. People say context counts for almost everything in a good drug trip, that, yes, the quality of the substance obviously matters, but that two pills of equal quality can result in totally different trips depending on if certain winning conditions are met.

You'll be ashamed you've never done molly before. If it was up to you, there'd never be a first time for anything. You wish you'd been born imbued with the sum of all human knowledge, because learning and discovering are shameful. They're proof you were once ignorant.

"If you do it," you'll say, "I'll do it."

"I'll do it," I'll say back with a smile, "if you do it."

We'll swallow our pills looking each other in the eye. Wash them down with a swig of beer.

What's incredible is that when the drug kicks in, you'll instantly know you've never felt happier.

What's sad, though, is that years later, you'll still say you never felt happier than at that moment. But you'll tell yourself that it's okay, that life's full of ups and downs, that life's a winding road and it's different for everyone. Then you'll tell yourself that maybe your life's the crest of a huge, exhilarating wave that you'll surf with me. But afterward, there'll be a backwash, a very long backwash that carries you far from shore, knocks you around, pulls you under. You'll tell yourself that even if one day another wave comes along, it'll never be as high as the first. You'll tell yourself that maybe the only thing left to do is accept that.

But at the time, none of that will be on your mind. No.

At the time, you'll look at me and a fire will break out. Neon will flow through your veins. Your head will float off your body. You'll see stars everywhere. You'll be amplified. Your skin will pick up every vibe, especially mine.

Your hand will touch my cheek. I'll materialize in front of you. And maybe I'll look like I might ask you what you're doing, but when I look into your eyes, I'll understand we're doing the same thing, that we're together, and I won't need to ask questions, so I'll go quiet and just gaze at you. You'll be exquisitely, incredibly, irrevocably happy—a perfect alignment of time, space, and me. Me.

We'll get lost in an ocean of sound and light. The rest of the night will turn liquid. Moments will flow together fluidly, time will go circular with no beginning or end. You'll float over the dance floor, the music and lights loosening gravity. At times, you'll realize you're in a parallel world, like when you order two drinks from the bartender and feel compelled to tell him he's absolutely gorgeous. We'll spend what could be a few minutes or a few hours, entwined, almost stock-still, in the middle of the crowd. You'll have to stop yourself from hugging me too hard, in case I break in two. Your face will hurt from smiling so much. You'll stop hugging me just so you can get a better look at me because you're stunned by how beautiful I am. You won't want to be anywhere else. You'll hear yourself say, "Will you marry me?"

I'll break into a smile, then burst out laughing. "Are you crazy?" I'll say. "No way!"

You'll force a laugh to turn your proposal into a joke. It wasn't a joke, though. The molly won't be enough to stop the wave of shame washing over you. Obviously I wouldn't say yes. You'll look away, gaze into the crowd, just long enough for you to imagine punching yourself in the face for making such a rookie mistake.

"Raph? I can't breathe!"

"What?"

"I can't breathe!"

"What can I do?"

"Get me outta here."

"No, we're having fun. Come on, let's stay."

"No, I told you I can't breathe. I gotta get out."

Even high as a kite, you'll understand you don't have the luxury to cross me, so you'll walk me to the lobby, holding my hand, and when we push open the door to outside, you'll realize time has passed much faster than you thought. Light will flood into the lobby like a dam bursting, and we'll step into a beautiful day, a bright blue sky, a sun that already came up a few hours earlier.

"Are you okay?" you'll say.

"Yeah, I just needed to get outta there."

"You can breathe now?"

"Yeah, yeah, I'm fine."

You'll pull me close, more to make sure I don't run off than to show me any real affection.

We'll head back to our Airbnb, stopping every two minutes to trip out on things we come across. We'll be like little kids. We'll point out the sky, the grass, all the buildings we pass, and we'll marvel at the beauty of the world.

Later, we'll end up in some ugly-ass neighbourhood we don't know, and you'll be too high to find it on Google Maps. We'll be in the street, you ahead of me, when you realize the molly's slowly wearing off. You'll turn to me. There I'll be, squinty-eyed, slack-jawed, hair a rat's nest, and you'll totally crack up, realizing how messed up I am from our night out. You'll ask me to stop a second so you can take my photo.

You'll frame me right in the middle. The sky in the background will be clear blue, picture-perfect, not a single cloud. Behind me will be an East German apartment building. My shoulders will be slumped, my face deathly pale.

You'll never delete that photo. At first, you'll look at it because you miss the girl in the picture. Later, you'll look at it because you miss the person who took the photo.

I DON'T HAVE ANY REAL EXPERIENCE IN COMEDY. I tried out a few bits at open mics just to test myself. I also auditioned for the comedy school (the same year as you, so we would've been in the same class, with Max Lap, Sam, André, Elena, and Thomas, and when I tell you that, you'll imagine an alternate universe in which we've become the power couple of comedy ever since our time at school). I didn't get in, but the jury did say I was a good writer, though my stage presence needed work. They suggested I come back and try out for the writing program. I never did. I got the job with Forand, and while I managed comedians with thriving careers, I put my own dreams on hold. When your job is to inflate other people's egos, even to monstrous proportions, there's not much room left for your own ego.

I'm okay with that. I'll always be okay with that. I'm not someone who generally has a lot of regrets. But you, you can't let it drop. You'll tell me over and over that it's a waste of my intelligence to put all my energy into writing emails and making sure Sam and the agency's other clients keep their appointments and meet their deadlines. This will be a good distraction. While you fret about my career, you can forget that your own has stalled ever since you got out of school and that it's not normal to always be late with your rent, whereas Sam has just put an offer on a condo and bought a new Subaru.

One Saturday morning at around eleven, you and me will be lazing around naked in bed and dissing a set we saw the night before. We'll cite all the reasons why the comic who did seven minutes on how to choose the right type of egg at the grocery store should be barred from every stage in Quebec. Together we'll list everything that should be banned in a comedy act: starting some observation about life with "have you ever noticed?"; any mention of cars, shopping, camping; telling the audience "Now, I know what you're gonna say" despite knowing they'll say nothing; and forty-seven other no-nos. We'll keep breaking into fits of laughter triggered by our mental symbiosis and by our surprise when we come up with even dumber comedy clichés. Then you'll straddle me, hold me down, tickle my ribs, but I'll fight back, shove you off, pummel you with a pillow. You'll catch your breath, look away, glance at the ceiling. Then say, "We really should be writing together."

The idea won't be so crazy. Our lives will already be so intertwined that we've lost track of exactly where I begin and you end.

Our brains have merged. When we're not having sex, we'll spend a lot of time together just watching movies and series and smoking weed, and you'll try discreetly to read any book I bring up to get over your complex of having a degree from the comedy school whereas I have a BA in literature, and we'll go to so many comedy shows together we can practically detect the germ of an idea in each other's brain even before the electric charge has time to travel from one neuron to the next and the idea can be verbalized. It'll take just a look, a tilt of the head, the simple contraction of a tiny muscle in the face for us to understand each other. Most times, this will be done to express anger or pass judgment. We'll never feel as united as when we have a common enemy: a dude who's too loud at a dinner, a girl who talks bullshit, or some loser comedian who laughs at his own jokes at a party. So no, us working together won't be such an outlandish idea.

By this point, we've been together for ten months. Your suggestion to team up will be even more intimate than your marriage proposal at Berghain. It's way easier to get divorced than to break a work contract, especially when it's never signed and is just an informal agreement.

You'll glance down at me. You looked away because it was embarrassing to make this suggestion. Even more embarrassing than telling me you love me. I'll take my time to answer. I'll seem to be thinking hard. As I go on thinking, hesitating, weighing the pros and cons, you'll realize you can't read me and that'll be crushing.

A serious tone in my voice, I'll finally say, "Okay."

I'LL FIRST PUSH YOU TO DEVELOP YOUR WEB PRESENCE.
"I know it's important," you'll say. "But I'm technologically challenged."

"No worries, I'll help you out," I'll tell you. "I can do a bit of video editing. I use Final Cut at the office to excerpt clips from our clients' shows and interviews. So if you come up with some crazy idea, just do a story. Who cares if it's not the joke of the century. At least it'll put you out there. Look at Max Lap, it put him on the map, right?"

"I'm game as long as I don't blimp out like him," you'll say. "You can get clicks without stuffing yourself with fried chicken."

You'll resurrect a character you created back in school—a foul-mouthed crossing guard. We'll shoot videos cheaply on the fly. We'll put a camera on a tripod in the middle of the street, and you'll try to do a few takes without getting arrested or run over. When you get a warning, you'll just move to another neighbourhood. It'll work out pretty good. Eventually you'll invest some money to rent better equipment and hire a skeleton crew.

You'll ask Max Lap and André to make cameos in your videos. Even though you hate grovelling to Sam, you'll ask him too. When you post a video where Sam plays a construction worker you butt heads with, you'll top a hundred thousand views. Sam will point out smugly that he pulled in a lot of those clicks.

I'll also ask Forand's big-name clients to make cameos. This will help, it'll give you a boost. Within months, you'll have a good ten thousand people following you on your YouTube channel and Facebook page.

Together we'll hit on the idea of filming tutorials. These will really take off. You'll create this know-it-all character, and we'll parody the kind of videos on makeup, renovations, cooking, and meditation found all over the web. These will go pretty viral.

I'll end up working on your stand-up too.

We won't set aside actual work sessions since our life together is a constant ping-pong of jokes. Our main challenge will be to take notes. On a trip to Charlevoix, you'll almost drive us off the road on the 138 when you try using your phone to write down a bit we think up on the photo shoots of real estate agents. You'll get bawled out once at a grocery store because you stop mid-aisle to take down an anecdote I tell you about my grandmother, who got way too nosy when my cousin came out as a lesbian.

Together we'll come up with some good material. In less than two months, we'll write at least two solid routines: a checklist of things to avoid in stand-up (too meta for a mainstream show, I'll say, but ideal for a comedy night in front of a more sophisticated audience) and a survival guide for dealing with old people (with jokes about my lewd grandmother and ways to liven up a visit to a decrepit great-aunt living in a nursing home).

Both bits will work great. You'll perform them ten times each at comedy clubs. One night, without warning, Thomas will come see you at a gig in Longueuil. He'll sit with a guy you don't know, a boomer who's a bit douchey and has a bone-crushing handshake and the voice of a he-man with four testicles.

"This is Daniel," Thomas will tell you. Daniel will shake your hand. "Hi, Raphaël," he'll say. "I'd like to set up a meeting so the three of us can discuss your first one-man show."

THE PRODUCER WILL HAVE AN OFFICE ON THE SOUTH Shore in Old Longueuil. Thomas will insist on driving you there because, though he may not be the best manager in town, he's very obliging. As you leave your apartment on the second floor and come down the stairs, he'll get out of his car and yell, "We have a winner!"

He'll jump on you, give you a noogie. You'll push him off, then lift him like a sack of potatoes to get your revenge.

"Stop, stop!" he'll cry. "You'll wrinkle my shirt!"

You'll put him down, and he'll carefully tuck his shirt back into his pants. He'll be wearing his blazer for special occasions, but with a floral-print shirt, something his girlfriend probably bought him at Simons for a wedding so he'd look suitably casual.

But today will be no casual event for Thomas. You'll be his first client to interest a producer. He can't wipe the smile off his face.

"I'm fucking proud of you, bro."

"Thomas, nothing's signed yet."

"No, but this is big. Enjoy it."

His car will look freshly washed as always. Two cold brews will sit in the cupholders between the front seats. The car's interior will reek of his cologne, something fresh, minty, herbal, which sounds good on paper but is a tad flashy. A fragrance that says, "Excuse me, I know I smell strong, but I'm here to show that my owner takes his personal hygiene seriously, and, by extension, he wants you to infer that he's a man who's conscientious, disciplined, in his element." Thomas has built much of his personality on his personal hygiene. This will make you think of my scent, which you then conjure up the same way someone might recall a song or a landscape. You can't help but smile. Seeing you smile, Thomas will also smile.

"I got you a cold brew since it's still pretty hot out. But if you want something else, we'll stop, okay? I didn't pick up any food. I figured we'd eat after, and anyway, I hate to eat before a meeting. We don't want food stuck between our teeth, right?"

Earlier that morning, while I was still half-asleep, I congratulated you, gave you a peck on the forehead. You told me this meeting was just as much my doing as yours. That made me smile.

"Working with Daniel is the best-case scenario," Thomas will say. "The guy's no cheapskate. He'll make sure the money goes where it needs to, you get exposure, and the venues are happy. Really, I think this could be good."

"Isn't your job to consider him a potential swindler?"

"My job's also to make sure you never have to worry about that stuff."

You'll arrive fifteen minutes early for your appointment. Thomas will drive around the block for exactly ten minutes. That way, you won't have to sit like idiots in some waiting room that might turn out to be uncomfortable, poorly air-conditioned, or badly soundproofed. Never let yourself absorb the vibe of a place that might potentially feel uninviting.

The building won't be that nice, but it'll be newly renovated and the furniture will look pricey. Maybe what matters most to producers for their office design is to look like they make enough money to afford an expensive space, but really they could work in an unfinished basement (since their job involves spending whole weeks on the phone and the price of their furniture has little impact on the success rate of their calls).

The receptionist will barely have time to say hello before Daniel comes out of his office. He'll shake your hand, give you an intense stare. Weirdly, he'll also lay a hand on your shoulder, a sort of paternal gesture.

"Really glad you agreed to come meet with me, man."

You'll throw Thomas a look that says, *Why wouldn't I agree? I've been dreaming of this for two years.* But Thomas won't notice since he's too busy drooling like a dog in front of Daniel.

"Come, come, let's go sit in the conference room. What do you take in your coffee?"

"No—"

"No, you already had one? So a decaf then? Sarah, a decaf. An espresso or a latte?"

"Just an espresso."

"A decaf espresso, Sarah."

The conference room will look out on a stretch of land and the river.

"The ex-wife got the cottage," Daniel will say with a laugh. "But I figure this view makes up for it."

Thomas will bark a fake laugh. You'll just smile stupidly.

"Hope you didn't mind having to cross the river."

"No, not at all," Thomas will say with a wave of his hand. "But this view almost makes me want to move here."

"Ha! Are you crazy?" Daniel will say with a grin. "No it doesn't."

You'll let out a laugh.

"But, of course, if you do a lot of touring," Daniel will

say, turning to you, "you might feel like moving to the South Shore. When you do gigs out of town, it's a lot less hassle not to have to deal with the bridges."

You'll shrug and say, "Uh, one thing at a time, I guess."

"I suggest you start planning soon. I have a feeling things are gonna take off pretty quickly for you."

Thomas will turn to you, enthusiastic, almost triumphant, and give you his I-told-you-so look.

"I saw you on that graduation tour you did with the comedy school. You were good, but still a bit academic or, I dunno, conventional maybe. You didn't necessarily have...a unique perspective, let's say. But I've seen you a couple times these past few months, and you've made real strides, man. Did any producers contact you when you got out of school?"

"Cambium approached him," Thomas will say. "But they didn't get his vibe. They kept saying that if they signed him, they'd cast him in one of their TV series, like some new drama on paramedics. But for them to suggest something like that shows they just really didn't get him. I mean, we can't just plunk Raph down in some drama series. That'd be so random."

"Ha! Anyway, Cambium's just a bunch of crooks. You don't wanna go there. They manage their agency like it's a Costco. They've got cheap merchandise and too much of it. Their TV series are crap, their comedy shows are crap, it's all crap."

You'll smile goofily. You never know if it's okay to bad-mouth people in these meetings. You always feel that there's no better way to make friends than to find a common enemy, but whenever you let loose and start ragging on a person, the target always turns out to be somebody's cousin's girlfriend and you cause some diplomatic incident. Still, Thomas will seem to know what he's doing, so you do what you rarely do—keep your trap shut.

"You're comfortable onstage," Daniel will say. "Even back in school, it was obvious you were legit. You have stage presence, no doubt about it, and that's good since it can't be taught. But I feel that recently you have more to say in your act. You go deeper, it's great. Your bit on what *not* to do in stand-up, it's pure gold."

"It's not too niche?" you'll ask.

Daniel will pause to think, gazing at the river. "Your little YouTube tutorials," he'll finally say, "they're kinda the same premise, right?"

"Yeah, I guess so."

"We'll just continue along those lines. It's a great place to start. A how-to guide on putting on a comedy show. Anyway, we can talk about it more, but one thing's for sure: you're ready for your first one-man show. I figure I'm not the only one chasing after you—"

"No, you aren't," Thomas will say over him. An obvious lie—Daniel will be the first producer to give any sign he knows you exist.

"Well, I can tell you I'd be very happy to produce you. It's now September, so we could reasonably start writing this fall whenever you're ready. If it's okay with you, we'd do previews in the spring, then the premiere just over a year from now. That'd leave us time to get you some more radio and TV exposure so people start recognizing you. You gotta be seen, Raph. That way, when the poster goes up, everyone'll know your face. So we have our work cut out for us."

"We'll have to check our schedule," Thomas will say. "But all in all, I'd say it sounds good. Anyway, we already have some material written."

"Who you wanna work with to write the show? I can team you up with somebody more senior, see how it works out. I've got Sylvain, who's a pro—"

"I already have a co-writer, and we work good together," you'll say. "I wrote my two routines with her."

"Oh, a woman to boot. Perfect. That way, we won't get accused of being a boys' club. You know how it is now. We can't work in peace anymore. We always have people telling us how to do our job. Anyway, who's the woman?"

"Laurie Blais."

"Hmm, never heard of her. Except that girl working for Forand. Isn't there a Laurie Blais there? It can't be the same girl. She'll have to use a pseudonym, otherwise it's confusing for everyone."

"She's pretty new on the scene," you'll say.

"Does she have the moxie to write a one-man show with a guy who hasn't got much experience?"

"We can still hook you guys up with a more experienced script editor," Thomas will say to me. "What do you think, Raph?"

"Um...yeah, sure. Why not."

"I already have an idea for a title," Daniel will say. "If we do the how-to guide, we might call it something like *How to Put on Your First One-Man Show*."

"It's not too long?" you'll ask.

"Maybe. I dunno. But it sure will stand out. Anyway, let's start by writing the show, then we'll see."

"I DON'T WANT YOU TO THINK I'M NOT TEMPTED. IT'S really not that."

You asked Thomas to let you off in front of Forand's office so you could steal me away for a coffee. (Of course, Thomas got all anxious, figuring you're stupid enough to openly shop around for another manager, even ask him for a lift there, just after you signed with a producer.)

"It's just that if I say yes, I'll have to quit my job at the agency, otherwise there'd be a conflict of interest. Besides, I wouldn't have time for both."

"Just quit. Isn't that what you want?"

"I don't know if I'm ready."

"What's holding you back? Money? You'd be totally fine for months with this contract. And if ever you're strapped, I'd help you out. Unless I got it all wrong, you don't plan on remaining Forand's assistant for the rest of your life."

"No, I know. You're right."

"Are you scared of working with me? Is that it?"

"No, I know we work well together. We're a perfect match."

"So why the hesitation?"

I won't reply at first. I'll slow my pace, stop, turn to you. I'm pretty hard to read, but you'll note a more troubled look on my face. You'll sense some looming disaster.

"You're so fucking gullible," I'll say. "As if I'd turn this down."

You'll give me a big grin. "I hate you!"

You were nervous enough that your armpits got a bit

sweaty and your heart rate went up. But now you'll have a good laugh, grab me, hold me in your arms. Like idiots, we'll both spill our coffees on the ground. We'll hug for what could be five seconds or five hours.

Finally, I'll let go and say, "This is great and all, but I wanna leave my job on good terms, so I'll need to give Forand two weeks' notice. After that, we can get to work."

"Okay by me. Now, since we'll have a professional relationship, I think we need to set some boundaries."

"Like what?" I'll say.

"I think we should stop sleeping together, otherwise it'll get too complicated."

I'll stifle a laugh. "Yeah, right. You wouldn't survive two days."

Two weeks later, we'll drive off to Eastman to stay at a cottage my aunt has kindly lent us for two weeks. ("The only thing I want in return," she'll say, "is tickets to opening night.") By the time we reach Ange-Gardien, we've already sketched out three bits and jotted down some decent jokes. We'll both be pretty wired, since Sam let you have some Ritalin from his stash.

I won't be on board with the Ritalin at first, but you'll say, "No use pretending that people in comedy can write a show sober. Or if they can, they don't go bragging about it all over town."

That'll convince me.

At first, my aunt's cottage will be so spotless we could eat off the floor. Twenty-four hours after we arrive, though, it'll look like an episode of *Hoarders*. We'll bring along enough food and booze to survive a zombie attack, but three-quarters of our groceries will remain in the entranceway, which turns into a sort of pantry. We'll leave empty boxes of frozen pizza and beer cans strewn everywhere—kitchen, living room, bedroom, den. We'll smoke outside at first, on the deck, but then gradually in the patio doorway, under the range hood, and finally anywhere at all. We'll get dressed and undressed whenever and wherever we want, till it's totally normal to find my panties lying next to the toaster. We'll revert to animals, and it'll be amazing.

Eight days will turn into one long day. We'll set the alarm for six a.m., get up, then pop a Ritalin and start work fifteen minutes later as it kicks in. We'll brainstorm and jot down our ideas without a break till we're hungry, which, because of the Ritalin, will happen much later than usual, typically around one p.m. We'll fuck while our breakfast cooks in the oven. We'll go back to work till the Ritalin starts wearing off, around six p.m. Then we'll start drinking, which slows our pace but leads to gags we couldn't write on Ritalin. When we get too incoherent, we'll roll a big joint and toke up while reading over the day's work, underlining the good stuff and crossing out the crap. Because you're stoned, your eyes will linger on my breasts, which look even more beautiful to you than usual, or I'll comment on your butt when I see you walking around naked in front of the huge windows overlooking the lake, and we'll fuck again. At this point, we might sleep a few hours, or we might not, who knows, but we'll see the sun come up again, and it'll be time to get back on the merry-go-round, take a Ritalin, reread with a clear head everything we wrote the day before, brainstorm, take notes, eat, fuck, joke around, rewrite, drink, chill, get a brilliant idea, write it down, develop it, smoke, fuck. It'll be one mad, thrilling vortex, and we'll emerge from it eight days later with a show made up of eight bits that are far from perfect, that are full of mistakes, that need rejigging, revising, refining, but still, eight bits that we can show to Sylvain, the script editor, and that you can start memorizing and practising so you can break them in at some comedy clubs to see if they hold up. We'll still have five days left to kill at the cottage. For the first time during our stay, we'll go out for a walk. The sun will burn our skin like we're vampires. We won't take Ritalin that morning, so for the first time in a long time, we can endure moments of silence that last longer than three seconds.

You'll gaze at the lake, squint from the sun. "I'm so fucking lucky to have met you," you'll say spontaneously. "I don't know what I'd do without you."

"You'd do okay on your own, I'm sure," I'll say. "Anyway, it's not so hard to write stand-up. Just take the right substances at the right time, and it writes itself."

"This isn't too healthy, though, is it?" you'll say.

"You wanna be healthy, or you wanna be interesting? Because you can't be both." I'll kiss you on the lips, then add, "I know what I wanna be."

"KNOW WHAT'S AWESOME? NOW THAT I'VE GIVEN YOU all my tips on putting on an excellent first one-man show, you don't need me anymore. You're fully autonomous!"

You'll look across the table in front of you, like a dog expecting a slap. You'll be too stressed out to read the room. Everyone might be disappointed in you, or impressed by you, or furious at you, they might've ignored you or been catatonic for an hour and a half, they might've been replaced by mannequins and you wouldn't know the difference. Your T-shirt will show dark rings of sweat in the armpits. During the table read, you couldn't take deep breaths, and only now that it's over can you relax your shoulders, release your diaphragm, take in more air. There'll be a moment of silence, and you can't tell how long it lasts. You'll glance at me to get my feedback, so I can tell you with one look if all went well or if you embarrassed me and tanked, but I'll be looking at Thomas, who'll be looking at Daniel, who'll be looking at Sylvain.

You'll start floundering. "The closer needs work. It was Laurie's idea. I wasn't a hundred per cent convinced, it's a good callback but not a gag per se, I don't know if it's strong enough to wow people before they head home, but still, I mean, it gives a general idea—"

"We can work with this," Sylvain will say.

Our pleading looks—mine, yours, Thom's, Daniel's—won't ease up any. People like Sylvain are hired for their taste, their ability to look at a comedy script and let the axe fall. They're paid a fortune to say yes or no. These taste-testers have one function: to react chemically to material to see if it's palatable to an audience or not. Any form of nuance or straying from a clear-cut, black or white answer is agonizing for those who rely on their judgment.

You'll jabber on: "It's definitely a work-in-progress, I mean, we haven't tested any of it on an audience, it's an idea really, just an idea..."

You'll picture Sam at the first table read of his show with Forand, and you'll wonder what kind of reaction he got, and it'll seem impossible, even though you wish it was true, that he could've gotten an uneasy silence or even a lukewarm reaction, and for a half second you'll want to get up, say, "Sorry, guys. Dunno what I was thinking," then back out of the rehearsal room, slam the door behind you, and run. In your mind, you'd have great stamina and could run at top speed for a long time, an hour almost, to get as far away as possible from this room, whereas we know that in reality you walk up two flights of stairs and you're out of breath.

"So the question right now, really, is does the idea hold up, does the concept work? If you don't like it, it's no big deal, we can go back to the drawing board no problem—"

"Raphaël, take a chill pill, man," Sylvain will say. "I said we can work with it."

You'll tilt your head, just a little, subtly, like a confused puppy.

"Jeez, did you graduate from the comedy school or fake your diploma?" Sylvain will go on. "It's like this is the first time you're breaking in material. Nobody's asking you to pull John Mulaney out of your ass. We just want an idea of the direction you're heading in."

You'll nod, mouth hanging half-open, like a hockey player trying to look smart when he's interviewed forty-five seconds after he comes off the ice.

Sylvain will turn to Daniel. "Dan, we can work with this, right?"

"Of course," Daniel will say with a smile. "I'm no dope. I knew he could deliver the goods."

A knot in your back will loosen. You could almost cry. "Oh. So you like it?" you'll say.

"Yep," Daniel will say. "It's exactly what we talked about. It's super funny, it's smart, it's different. You have your own style. It's just the kind of show I want."

"Of course, it's gonna evolve," Thomas will add. "We'll break it in."

"Yeah, yeah," Daniel will say. "We know that, but I think it's great."

You'll feel very weak all of a sudden. Like a bus sped by in the street, just missing you because someone pulled you back onto the sidewalk in the nick of time.

Like I was the one who instinctively pulled you back, saved you from yourself.

"Smoke break, then notes afterward," Sylvain will say. He'll wave four big sheets of paper covered in scribbles. "I've got all these notes for you guys. That's a good sign."

That evening, when we get back to my place, you'll burst into tears as you come through the door. I'll help you to bed and rub your back awhile till you can catch your breath and speak.

"You okay?" I'll say softly.

"Yeah, yeah."

"Did something bad happen?"

"No, no."

"Do you have regrets about the show?"

"No, not at all."

I'll kiss your cheek and hold you tight for what seems to you like a half-hour. We'll then lie back, hold hands, stare at the ceiling. Your breathing will slow. You'll gradually return to a more or less normal state and have a sort of afterglow that's not necessarily unpleasant.

Eyes averted from me, you'll say, "When people like me, I sometimes feel it's all a joke."

I'll roll onto my side. You'll do likewise, then look me in the eye without speaking.

"Why would it be a joke?" I'll ask.

It'll cross your mind to admit you don't deserve what's happening to you, that you feel unworthy—unworthy of the show, unworthy of me—and that you figure I probably would've despised you if we'd met back in high school when you were the poster boy for incels. It'd do you a lot of good to admit that. Even if your entire artistic approach involves creating a larger-than-life persona who's cool-headed, mouthy, destructive, even if mockery is your Olympic sport, even if you're mean and nothing surprises you and people can spit venom at you and it drips off, water off a duck's back or, better yet, you spit it right back with even better aim and make everyone around you laugh, it'd still do you a lot of good to tell me that you can never totally believe that people like you, that you feel like Carrie at the prom, that everybody's playing a prank on you. It'd do you a world of good, but you can't bring yourself to say it.

Instead, you'll just say, "No reason."

You'll wonder what would've happened if you'd had the balls to let your guard down. You'll wonder that for the rest of your life.

YOU WON'T SEE ANY WARNING SIGNS.

You can't pinpoint when things go south. It'll be like I just wake up one morning and stop loving you. That won't be what happens of course. It's never like that. But, though you'll try hard, you can't fathom any other possibility. It'll hit you like a bus might hit you one morning when you cross the street. Life can change fast, can change in an instant. You'll get in a car to go to Gatineau and the life you knew will be over.

To try to understand, you'll replay the film in your head, minute by minute, since the start of our relationship, wondering how and why things went off the rails. And, later, when you want to erase those memories from your head, there'll be no way you can. You've stared at that film so long the images will be seared into your brain.

The end especially. The end you'll know by heart. Every second. It'll be a weekend in late May. We'll pack the car like it's a game of Tetris because we take Thomas and Max Lap along when we drive to Gatineau where you'll do two previews. (Max will be both your technical director and opener. The web got sick of his fried chicken faster than he did, so with his YouTube career petering out, he'll now go back to being a stand-up.)

You'll die an old man, but even at the end of your life, you'll remember what happens next.

You'll accidentally spill a coffee on me when we stop for takeout before picking up Thomas and Max.

"What's your fucking problem?" I'll yell.

The hot coffee will be pretty unpleasant, yes, and probably burn, but you'll find my reaction overblown. In my face, you'll see a violence you've never seen before—or you've seen only once, a week earlier. That other time, you've been on tour a week and miss me because you have to sleep all alone in hotels. So you'll be eager to fuck again when you get back. And even though we'll sometimes play rough, I might bite you or ask you to spank me, or you might manhandle me a bit for fun, get a little kinkier but not too much, even though we'll sometimes do that, this time, after not seeing you for a week, which isn't so long really, I'll kick it up a notch. I'll bite you hard, harder than usual, and my fingernails will dig deep into your arms and back, and while we're kissing, I'll bite your tongue. You'll try to catch my eye to show that, no, that's not the mood you're after, that you just want to make love normally, but you won't catch my eye because I'll look away, and when you lose patience and try to play my game, by gripping my jaw to force me to look at you, you'll see a violence in my eyes you've never seen before. It'll scare you. You'll still cum, you'll always cum, the problem's not there. The problem's that when you look in my eyes, you'll realize I've become someone else. You'll realize I've turned into someone who doesn't love you anymore.

Afterward, we'll get caught up in our work and planning our little road trip, and you'll banish the incident to a dark corner of your mind you don't visit too often. We need those dark corners to hide the bad feelings we get, otherwise no one could go on living.

"What's your fucking problem?"

The look on my face, and the pause after my question, will tell you it's not a question but an insult: *You have a problem. You deserve to be shot.*

The tears will start in your solar plexus and rise fast, but you'll block them in your throat, and they'll turn into an apologetic smile. "I'm really sorry," you'll say.

Normally, you'd be fuming, but this time, you'll just be hit by a big wave of sadness. You'll know you can't afford any more mistakes. You've had two strikes and won't want a third.

You couldn't afford a single strike, in fact. You knew it as soon as you came up to me earlier tonight and suggested we do shots. But people are great at telling themselves fairy tales. They're great at forgetting they know when a story will end badly.

You'll wonder whether to defuse the situation, to gently suggest I stay in Montreal and come see you at another gig to give you my notes on our script. But you'll quickly realize it wouldn't look good to suddenly leave me in the lurch, so you'll drop that idea.

All the muscles in your body will tense. You'll smile. "I really am sorry," you'll say.

The tension will fester and grow in the silence of the car, but once we pick Thomas up, we'll manage to pretend to be a relaxed, happy couple ready for their road trip. I'll be talkative, funny, clever. I'll know how to fire up the car with just the right playlist playing in the background to create a party vibe and loosen things up. Thomas will compliment me, tell me I'm an amazing co-pilot. It'll make you sad to hear that.

We'll talk shop, of course we'll talk shop. We can't not. Normal people have their work and play, they have interests, they're out in the world carrying on real conversations, but us, no, of course not. We'll spend the whole drive talking about somebody's shitty act, somebody else's fierce radio appearance, the wack choice of hosts for the award galas this year, your preview run (which is going great), the one-man show itself (which will kill, everyone agrees, even though you've still got work to do). This shoptalk will suit you fine because it'll let you take part in a conversation with me. That'll seem important to you because you believe, and rightly so, that this is one of our last conversations as a couple.

YOU'LL FEEL LIKE YOU NEED TO GET CLOSER TO ME. Physically closer.

Just after we enter our hotel room and put down our bags, you'll come up behind me and kiss my neck.

I'll jump out of my skin. Without thinking, I'll slap you in the face. "Sorry," I'll say, "but...you startled me."

I won't look guilty in the least. When I apologize, I won't even look you in the eye. I'll go lock myself in the bathroom. You'll hear a rustling as I strip off my clothes. Then a squeal from the plumbing as I turn on the shower. I'll disappear behind the sound of running water.

You can't move. You'll stand stock-still in the middle of the room staring at the bathroom door, shoulders hunched, mouth filling with saliva, stomach queasy. There'll be a weakness in your chest, a chill slowly spreading throughout your body. A feeling of imminent death.

Thomas will knock on the door to our room. He'll save you from the ordeal of having to pick up where we left off once I'm out of the shower.

"We gotta get to the theatre for the sound check, Raph," he'll say.

You'll try to convey something to him with your look, but he won't catch on. Thomas never catches on.

"Laurie's still in the shower." You'll turn to the bathroom door and say louder, "We gotta get going, Laurie."

"I'll grab a cab and meet you there," I'll yell.

You'll want to mention something to Thomas in the car,

but you'll realize you have nothing concrete to say. What should you say? That I wasn't in the mood to fuck when we got to the hotel? That you thought I was rude to you on the way there? As long as you don't talk about the end of the world out loud, maybe it'll never happen. Some people can go on for years like that. You'll tell yourself you'd rather carry on like that for years than accept I'm leaving you. If you had to choose, you'd rather be unhappy with me than happy without.

"The sound check should be over by around three o'clock. You have an interview at the theatre with Radio-Canada Gatineau at three thirty. After that, we have Rouge FM at four thirty by phone, which we can do in the car. Then Cogeco at five ten, but that one's in the studio."

"Okay."

"I did your Facebook post and put the promo on Insta as a story. If you could do a story or two before six, that'd be great too. Something nutty. Daniel would like that because there are still tickets to sell for tomorrow."

"A lot of tickets?"

"No, no, but he'd like to say during the day tomorrow that the show's sold out. It'd look good. Try doing something wacky, like maybe pretend you're gonna perform before Parliament."

"Okay."

"Have you started working on your radio piece? Remember you're on Énergie FM on Monday."

"Yeah, I know. It's all good."

"And you should get to a barber before you go on *Le Tricheur* on Thursday."

"Oh, shit."

"It's your first time on the show, so why not make a good impression."

"I thought you said I shouldn't look *too* good."

"Yeah, but don't look homeless either. I'll book the barber near your place. You won't have to call."

"I fucking hate game shows."

"Back when no one knew your name, you would've sucked ass to get on a frigging game show, so don't go moaning about it now."

You'll have that feeling, the one where you know something super bad will happen, but you can't do anything to avert it. It's like the last few seconds before impact in an airplane crash.

In a gentler voice, Thomas will say, "Everything okay, bud?"

"Yeah, yeah. I just need a coffee, I guess. Maybe I didn't get enough sleep."

"I'll get you one while you get settled in the green room."

You'll manage to paste on a smile as you walk into the theatre. Back in school, after nights of heavy drinking with classmates, you learned you can force yourself up onstage no matter what. Even if you're so hungover you want to puke your guts out. Even if you've just had one arm hacked off. Even if you're at death's door. And no one would be the wiser.

After the sound check, Thomas will be waiting for you in the green room with a lukewarm espresso.

"It's from the bar in the theatre. If it's awful, tell me and I'll find you another one. Is there any good coffee in Gatineau? If not, no worries, I'll get you one on the other side of the river, end of story."

You'll sip the espresso, which is truly gross. "It's fine," you'll say. "Anyway, I just wanted the caffeine."

"Need anything else?"

"No, I'm good. The fridge is full. I've got my backstage beer."

"Great, bro."

"You didn't have to come spend the whole weekend with us, y'know."

"Yeah, but I haven't seen the show in weeks. And it's nice to get away from Montreal. Plus my girlfriend's coming by train tomorrow to meet me for a little getaway. Neither of us has ever visited Parliament."

Thomas is the kind of guy who might have trouble remembering the prime minister's name. He'll glance at his phone. "Okay, we're on. Radio-Canada is all set up in the theatre. You'll do the interview sitting on the edge of the stage. It'll look awesome with the screens in the background and the lighting."

Thomas will guide you through the theatre's maze of pitch-dark corridors. Your face will be hot, and you'll feel like you might pass out. "Have you seen Laurie?" you'll ask him.

"She must be on her way."

The route you take is winding and endless, but you'll finally emerge backstage, then onto the stage. A reporter, who's even younger than you, will be waiting. Beside her, a guy shaped like a trucker will be holding a camera with the Radio-Canada logo on it.

"Hello, Raphaël," the reporter will say and shake your hand. "I'm Audrey and I'll be doing your interview. It'll be fairly short, a three-minute piece airing on tonight's newscast."

"There are no small reports, only small TVs." You could shoot yourself for making such a lame joke, but still the reporter will burst out laughing. This is something you've already learned, but your experience in the coming years will confirm it: being funny is way easier than we think. We vastly overestimate the intelligence of the public and reporters.

That's why Sam is such a success. And it's why you often have to fight the temptation to be as lowbrow as he is. But, together, you and me will manage to create comedy that's just a bit more sophisticated.

Audrey will give directions to the cameraman, who curses the theatre's lighting and grumbles that he can't properly frame you if you sit on the edge of the stage. Then she'll step in front of you, all enthusiastic, and look you in the eye with a hunger that might be more than just professional.

"Raphaël, almost no one had heard of you a year ago, but today you've made a mark, thanks in part to your YouTube channel where some of your sketches have topped a million views. What's made them such a hit?"

"To tell you the truth, the trick was just to stop questioning myself. With my videos, I can try some dumb stuff in the heat of the moment without censuring myself. A little like when I did improv back in high school. Everything basically starts from there."

"And that spawns characters like your crazy crossing guard. He behaves badly, insults kids, gets into a fight with an old man."

You'll snort a laugh like you've been caught behaving badly yourself. "Yeah, yeah, that's my guy," you'll say.

"And even though you started doing stand-up in clubs after leaving the comedy school, it's these YouTube videos that helped you land your first solo show, which you're previewing for us tonight."

"That's right."

"So what changed between the Raphaël of a year ago and the Raphaël we see today?"

"Not much, except now people wanna hear my stupid jokes."

"You've worked closely with a scriptwriter, Laurie Blais, for some time now. What's her role in all this?"

You'll glance at Thomas, who isn't listening, just staring at his phone.

"Laurie Blais? Laurie's a great collaborator, but she just helps out now and then. We sometimes bounce ideas off each other, but that's all. No, it's really just because I decided to change direction a year ago and launch my YouTube channel. Everything took off from there. Basically, I owe my success to the people who follow me online."

"Raphaël Massicotte, thank you!"

It'll be four o'clock, then five, then six, and still no word from me. The interviews will all be a pain in the ass, but at least they'll keep your mind almost completely occupied till it's time to go onstage.

By this point in your career, you've tamed the beast. You'll know how to calm your nerves before you go onstage. You'll drink two pints, joke around awhile with the other comics in the green room (Max Lap during this tour), then head backstage to watch the show about ten minutes before you go out, all the while trying to slow down your breathing as best you can. Everything's in the breathing. Relaxing the diaphragm. The difference between a gag that lands and a gag that tanks sometimes comes down to this one muscle.

As your opener, Max Lap will deliver a strong set, like he always does. He's dropped his more suburban material, like his cheesy bit on all-inclusive resorts, worthy of Jimmy Fallon, to focus on anecdotes he's gathered while travelling the world and eating like a pig. His act will be different, and it'll speak to people. By this point, Max will weigh two hundred and fifty pounds, so the guy has serious stage presence. His big body will be a big sound box for his big voice.

When you hear his bit on how he, a fat white dude, tried protecting his personal space in the Tokyo subway, you'll know he's got about two minutes left in his set.

As usual, you'll close your eyes tight. Take a deep breath. You'll tell yourself nothing bad can happen.

You'll remember the last time you told yourself nothing bad could happen. You'll see my face, just as you see it now, tonight, in André's kitchen. You'll replay the movie of your day. Me giving you hell as we leave for Gatineau. Me backing away when you want to make love. Me disappearing behind the bathroom door.

"Raaaaaaaaaaaph Massi!"

You won't hear Max Lap's closer. Or the crowd applauding. Or the recorded voice announcing your name. You'll be too focused on clenching your jaw to hold back a sob. It'll work, but you'll go out onstage a few seconds late. Obviously no one will notice. But you'll notice. It'll be enough to throw you off. And performing stand-up is a balancing act demanding perfect control.

"Hey, I'm glad to be in Gatineau tonight. Y'know, it's a real treat for me to be here because I'm a big fan of a lot of Gatineau celebrities. Like my favourite of all is that redneck who went viral when he bragged on the news about turning his property into an illegal landfill."

Crickets from the crowd.

You'll get back on track and turn things around, but you'll feel off, almost out of breath. Still, you'll get laughs, of course you'll get laughs. Many of your bits will already be tried and tested, and you can practically deliver them with your eyes shut, on autopilot, knowing when to raise your voice, when to pause a beat, when to shift your gaze to a certain spot. But autopilot isn't doable for an entire show. The audience knows when you're not a hundred per cent present, when you're stuck in your own head. They don't necessarily understand what's wrong. For ninety minutes, they can watch a decent comic who moves fluidly onstage, tells well-written jokes, has good delivery and timing, and they figure they should be enjoying themselves, but, without knowing why, they're bored senseless.

You'll be missing just one thing: a spark in your eyes. A fire that people can see but can't quantify. They only realize it exists when it's gone out. That's what people mean when they say you're good onstage and can get audiences eating out of your hand in no time. You can meet them at their level, act as their guide, lead them gently by the hand into your world. You get them to listen to you, follow you anywhere. And, ideally, you also get them laughing.

You'll be doing the part of the show where you list everything you hate in stand-up and slag the whole concept of puns. There'll be a half second when you step out of your spotlight a little as you move around the stage. It'll be just enough time to see the audience a bit better. Enough time for you to wonder where I'm sitting and what I think of the show. Whether I despise you. Whether I think you suck. Whether I cooled on you because I basically realized everything you do is shit, that you're talentless, ugly, that I'm wasting my time with you.

You obviously can't see where I'm sitting. And you'll realize, during the half second you're thinking of me, that you've lost your train of thought. You'll be a deer and the audience will be speeding toward you at two hundred kilometres an hour.

83

We lose all sense of time onstage, so you can't really tell how long it'll last, this gap during which the only sound will be your frantic breathing coming out of the theatre's speakers. Then the rustle of somebody fidgeting in their seat. Then a discreet cough. Then three more coughs at the same time.

You'll repeat what you've just said: "So, y'know, some comics still figure it's perfectly alright to toss out a bad pun onstage..."

It's not like you memorize your script word for word. The transitions occur naturally whenever you tell a story onstage. There's no manual for situations where the link holding ideas together in a coherent whole suddenly snaps and you're left totally exposed before a thousand people who came out to laugh but unfortunately end up feeling *pity* for an amateur who misjudged his ability to deliver the goods.

Three seconds? Ten seconds? A minute? Three hours?

You'll think of a pianist I once told you about who composed a piece called *Four Minutes* (or *Four Minutes* something, you can't remember the exact title). You'll think of that piece, which is actually four minutes and several seconds of silence performed onstage in front of an audience that grows increasingly restless and noisy, becomes itself the music.

This won't help you get back on track. You'll realize you never heard about this piece before I told you about it. You'll tell yourself I'm smarter than you. You'll wonder if you'll regress intellectually once I'm gone.

"I'm so fucking sorry, guys."

The audience will give you a round of applause as a sign of support.

Feeling wrung out, you'll improvise. "Is it just me or does it smell like burnt toast in here?"

Out of sympathy, the crowd will force a laugh. Your brain

fart will suddenly dissipate and you'll remember what you're supposed to say. "Want a bad pun?" you'll ask the crowd. "The present, the past, and the future walk into a bar. It's tense." A play on words so corny everyone will laugh.

I'm the one who suggested you make fun of puns so you can get away with slipping a few dad jokes into your act. Audiences eat that shit up.

You'll recoup and manage to finish the gig like it's any other. What'll be different, though, is that after the overly generous applause and your bow, you'll head offstage with a desire to put a bullet through your brain.

And even if Max Lap gives you a big hug back in the green room and Thomas brings you a beer and tells you that it was nothing, that blanking onstage is horrible the first time it happens but it happens to everybody, your desire for that bullet won't fully go away.

You'll need me to come tell you that your slip-up was actually funny, that it lasted three seconds at most. But I'll just send you a text saying I'm tired and that I went straight back to the hotel after your performance.

When you join me there, you'll ask, "How did you like the show?"

"You were perfect," I'll say.

"Perfect?"

"Yeah."

"No notes?"

You'll hold back a sob, a muffled sound that stays caught in your throat.

"You didn't come."

I'll just shake my head.

"I fucking blanked onstage."

"It happens."

85

"The real problem's not that."

You won't want to get into it. You'll plead with yourself not to, but you'll feel so bursting with despair that the words slip out. "What's going on, Laurie?"

And even though you could be referring to anything—the bedsprings squeaking in the next room where people are fucking, the siren blaring outside—even though your question is super vague, I'll understand exactly what you mean.

"I dunno," I'll say gravely.

"Are you thinking of breaking up?"

"I dunno."

The most affirmative "I dunno" you've ever heard in your life.

You'll suddenly need to get away from me. There'll be no other option. But you'll stupidly leave our hotel room in just your boxers. You'll be out in the overly bright corridor feeling totally drained. You'll stumble past the dirty room-service trays left on the floor, your breathing strained, your throat tight, your jaw clenched. You'll catch a glimpse of yourself in a mirror in the corridor and remember that you don't look so hot bare-chested. Maybe if you'd tried going to a gym, *maybe*, just maybe, it would've made a difference and convinced me to stay with you.

With each step, it'll become harder to contain the blaze burning in your belly. Your chest will start heaving, your shoulders shaking. You'll hunch over. Your knees will buckle, so you'll have to lean against the wall to keep from falling down. Eventually, though, you can't hold yourself up. It'll feel to you like someone has stabbed you in the guts with a bayonet. A guttural sound will fill the corridor, so grotesque it takes you a few seconds to realize it's coming from you.

I'll pull on a T-shirt and pyjama bottoms and go after you.

I'll head down the hallway and find you in front of the elevator. You'll be on all fours crying like a baby. You'll try to speak but just let out a wail. A long string of drool will run from your mouth to the carpet.

"Raph, Raph, stop it! This is ridiculous. You're gonna wake everyone up."

You'll find it hard to speak. Your crying will twist your mouth into a horrible grimace. You can't enunciate, but after several attempts, I'll finally understand what you're trying to say: "Why are you doing this to me?"

"Raph, can we just...not do this here?"

You'll try getting up but fall back down. I'll consider leaving you there but end up pulling you to your feet. You can't support your own weight, so I'll help you back to our room like you're a wounded soldier.

In front of our door, I'll say, "Can you open it? I don't have my card."

"I didn't bring mine either," you'll say, half-sobbing.

"Fuck."

You'll lean your forehead against the door, then slide to the floor, your chest heaving up and down. You'll be racked by violent sobs, almost howls, then curl up in a ball like an animal in front of the door.

I'll stand staring at you. How long? Three seconds, ten seconds, a minute, three hours? Time will be as loose as when you froze onstage.

You won't see me leave. When I get back, you'll still be crying, but at least not as loud.

I'll have two key cards with me. "Here," I'll say, giving you one. "I got a room for myself."

You won't have the strength to reach up to open the door with the card.

"You okay, sir?"

Time has passed, you won't know how much, but a hotel employee will be squatting down in front of you. Your face will be all puffy, and you've made a wet spot on the carpet from drooling.

"Do you have your room key?"

You'll manage to move a finger to point to the key card on the floor beside you. The employee will pick it up, slide the card into the lock, give you the card back. You'll crawl into your room.

"I know it may not mean much right now," the dude will say, "but I really like what you do." He'll close the door behind you.

You'll lie down in the entrance to your room and spend the night on the floor.

THE REST OF THE WEEKEND WILL BE ONE BIG CHARADE.
The four of us will go for brunch—you, me, Max Lap, and
Thomas. The guys will tease you about blanking onstage, but
in a good-natured way. Sam would've savaged you, but Max
Lap's a sweetheart and Thomas knows it's not in his interest to bruise your ego. When Thomas has notes for you, I'll
make up stuff to add. He'll agree with me since I'm a good
bullshitter. No one will catch on. And since I'm pretending
everything's A-okay, you'll be forced to play along.

You'll spend the rest of the day staring at the ceiling of your
room after claiming to Thomas that you need to write your
radio piece for Monday.

Thomas's girlfriend will come to the second show,
on Saturday night. The five of us will go out for dinner
afterward, then for a drink, like it's any normal Saturday.
Thomas's girlfriend will tell you and me that we make an
awesome couple. She'll say you were fantastic onstage and
compliment me on the writing of the show. Hearing this,
you'll want to die.

On Sunday, we'll pack the car even more tightly than on
the way up. You'll try hard not to cry on the drive back from
Gatineau. Once we drop Thomas and his girlfriend off at his
place, you'll think we're finally going to talk, but I won't say
a word. I'll just stare out the window in silence. And you'll be
tempted to take another route, to drop me off at my apartment
first, to say, "I'm letting you off at your place since it's over
between us," but you won't have the courage or the energy.

All your life force will be spent holding back your tears.

We won't say a word to each other. You'll park in front of your place. You'll open the trunk, we'll take our suitcases out. We'll go upstairs, put our suitcases down. Only then will I turn to you and say, "We have to talk."

"So it's happening, right?" you'll say.

"Yes, it is."

You won't be surprised, but still, my words will roll over you like a tractor-trailer. You'll start salivating. You'll hurl your tote bag on the floor but then realize your MacBook is in it. (It'll later cost you eight hundred bucks to replace the screen. You'll go teary-eyed in front of the Apple Store guy. You'll say, "My girlfriend left me, so I smashed my screen." It won't be funny, just cringe.)

You'll ask me, "So what's up with us?"

"I just...I want us to stop seeing each other."

The San Andreas fault will crack open.

"Why?"

The Twin Towers will collapse.

"I don't love you anymore, Raph."

Chernobyl will melt down.

"But why?"

An asteroid will hit, wiping out all life on Earth.

"It's just...I don't love you anymore."

"I need a reason, Laurie. Give me a reason."

"You know things don't work that way."

"There's a reason. There's a reason you decided to go home with me that night at André's."

"Raph—"

"And there's a reason you're telling me this now. There's always a reason." As you say this, you'll come closer, grab me by the shoulders. I'll slowly back away till I'm up against the

90

living-room wall. You won't let go of my shoulders. You aren't gripping hard, no, but still you'll have your hands on me and your face a few inches from mine, and if you asked me how I feel then, I'd say I feel scared. Terrified even.

"Have I just been a pity fuck from the start?" you'll say.

"Raph, I...I just can't go on like this, okay?"

"Is it because you wanna see other guys?"

"No—"

"If you wanna see other guys, we can work something out, Laurie. I can be flexible. If you tell me you want some compromise, I can deal. All I want is to keep you—"

"Raph, that's not it."

"I just want you to stay with me. Tell me what I can do for you to stay with me and I'll do it."

Later, you won't remember any of this. Your mind will erase almost the whole conversation. For a variety of reasons.

Your grip on my shoulders will loosen. Your face will gently lower to my chest. You'll wither, lean your head against me. Your temple will be burning hot.

"I can't live without you. I've never loved anyone else, Laurie. Not like this. Never."

"Raph—"

"I was nothing before you. Everything I have in life, I owe to you. My career, this apartment, just the fact I'm *alive*, it's because of you—"

"Raph, stop. Just...stop, okay?"

You'll slide limply down my body till you lie like a blob at my feet. I'll stare at you a long time, then say, "I'm gonna go, okay?"

"So that's it then. You're leaving and that's it."

"No, no..."

"Yeah, that's it."

A pause. Then you'll say, "What are we gonna do about the show?"

I'll take a deep breath. "The show's fine, Raph," I'll say warily. "We spent the weekend discussing it. I can come back this summer to tweak things if you want, but...the show's gonna be good. I'm not worried about it at all."

"We won't work together."

"We can talk about it later—"

"I couldn't do it."

"Okay, Raph. Fine."

A crack will open up in you, starting from your sternum. A torrent of lava will rise from your chest to your face. You'll start to cry, then emit a wail. You'll crawl to the opposite corner of the living room.

"But I need you. I need you to stay with me."

I'll open my mouth, my lips will start to form words that I end up holding back. You'll become hyperaware of your surroundings. A cop car will drive by in the street. The wind will rustle the leaves outside.

You'll breathe hard, body convulsing, sobs coming out of your mouth. I'll move toward you but back off when you scream, "Get away from me!"

You'll stay sitting there in the corner, your back against the wall. You'll stare at me, I'll stare at the floor.

"Can you get me my smokes?" you'll finally say.

I'll stand there a moment, then take your pack of cigarettes from your bag. I'll come over, lay it in front of you like an offering to some dangerous beast. I'll back away.

You'll light a Benson, watch me slowly disappear behind a cloud of smoke as you absorb the little bit of comfort the nicotine provides.

"I still think we could work together again," I'll say

tentatively. "At some point down the line."

"I don't want you working with me out of pity."

"Plenty of people manage to work together even after a breakup."

"Yeah, but I love you, Laurie. I fucking love you. I don't think you get that."

"Raph—"

"I know you're way out of my league. I know it makes no goddamn sense that we were together and I should be grateful for even having spent a single day with you, but—"

"That's not true—"

"I never felt I belonged anywhere till I met you."

"Don't say that—"

"But it's true. It's so true. You think I'm bullshitting? It's fucking true! Let me say it!" You'll try lowering your voice, but you can't. As you speak, you'll alternate between shouting, crying, and panting. "I love you for real, Laurie," you'll say. "Like I've never loved anyone else. So no, I don't think we can keep working together. Not if I want to survive this."

Something in my eyes will tell you I'm tempted to correct you, tell you you'll survive, that you're safe because no one dies from a broken heart. But my fear will win out, so I'll just say, as a kind of truce, "Okay then."

You'll pitch forward, bury your face in your hands. "Is there someone else?" you'll mutter.

"No, it's not that."

"So the problem's just me."

Your reaction would probably be the same if I told you there *was* someone else. The reason won't matter. What'll hurt is that there *is* a reason to leave you.

Realizing that will be like ripping out a fish hook lodged in your belly, but without the relief of finally removing the source of the pain. The pain will still be there, and it won't go away.

You'll start crying again. You'll cry so much you can't catch your breath and your abs hurt.

"Do you want me to..." I won't finish my sentence. What can I actually do? Call an ambulance? Call your mom? Call Sam? My pause will seem to last five minutes, maybe ten, but then I'll finally say, "I'm...I'm gonna go now."

"It's crazy, though, isn't it?" you'll manage to say.

"What?"

"I'm a bachelor now, all alone in my bachelor pad."

I won't know how to respond. After a while, I'll say, "Okay, this time I'm going for real."

I once said the same thing to you at the start of our relationship: "This time I'm going for real." I was kissing you over and over in the doorway. I'd be late for work because we couldn't let go of each other. Thinking about that will make you start crying even harder.

When people are in the hospital, they're asked to rate their pain on a scale of one to ten, ten being the most intense they've ever felt. For the rest of your life—through appendicitis, a bike accident, two car accidents, two concussions, and various infections—you'll never feel such acute pain again. What you'll feel that day becomes your standard for a ten out of ten.

"THAT STORY DOESN'T MAKE YOU LOOK SO GOOD," you say.

We've been talking for a half-hour, both of us leaning against the kitchen counter. We're quite a bit drunker now, so you aren't as self-conscious with me. Behind us, in the living room, twenty people are dancing, jumping in place, yelling. André hurries down the hall in a panic. In the entranceway, the upstairs neighbour stands with his arms crossed, looking irate, arguing about the noise with Max Lap. Sam's in the hall chatting up some random girl.

The humidity has begun to bead on the ceiling. Any time now, little droplets may start falling on our heads.

"You think this makes me look bad?" I ask.

"Well, you don't come off as a nice person."

"It's not nice to fall out of love with someone and say so?"

"Hmm, if you put it that way..."

You take a swig of your beer, look me in the eye. You can't help smiling. You even stifle a laugh.

When you look me in the eye, you get a feeling inside, a warm, velvety, tingly feeling everywhere. You almost never look anyone in the eye too long. It's hard. It's hard but so worth it.

"What?" I ask, amused.

"Nothing, nothing. It's just...you're kinda weird."

"I try. Like I said earlier, I wanna be a writer."

"Well, you're pretty good at telling scary stories."

I point to the balcony door. "Wanna grab a smoke?" I say. "I'm suffocating in here."

"Sure, sure."

"The sweat of all you young comics is dripping into my beer. It's grossing me out."

You start off toward the balcony, but I lay a hand on your forearm to stop you. My touch burns your skin. The heat courses to your belly. Your throat contracts, your breathing slows. You get an instant hard-on.

This is the first time we've touched. You don't know if the touch is pure reflex on my part or betrays my intent to get closer to you. But it sure feels good. It feels *so* good. You want me to cover every inch of your skin with my body.

"What's gonna happen now," I say, "is we'll go outside and see Elena Miller getting fucked in the alley."

"You know Elena?"

"No, but I do know she was in school with you, that you bang her twice a year, and that she was betting tonight would be one of those nights. But unfortunately for her, you've got other plans, so she's making do with her new boyfriend, the himbo."

You let out a laugh, and I pull you toward the door. "C'mon," I say.

When we step outside, it's like a thermal shock since the change in temperature is so great. It's also like climbing out of a pond because the air inside is so humid and rank.

"Look down there," I say.

You have to hold back a laugh when you glance toward the alley.

"Shh!" I say.

You recognize Elena's big mane of curly hair, her head bowed, her arms up against a telephone pole. Behind her is her dude, his long, tattooed arms, his hands grasping her waist, his naked ass thrusting, his head tilted back, his panting breath echoing off the surrounding fences and forming little clouds of condensation whenever he exhales.

You look at me, disconcerted. "How do you do it?"

"Do what?"

"How do you *know*?"

I give a sad little smile. "I can't reveal my sources," I say.

You want to dig deeper but don't dare in case I back off or find you too intense or intrusive, so instead, you just stare at Elena in the alley. "I don't wanna keep watching, but I can't *not*," you say.

"I know, right?"

"I didn't necessarily wanna see that douche fucking."

"Dumb-ass seems to know what he's doing, though."

That gets another laugh out of you. You cover your mouth with your hand so they won't hear.

"Y'know, no matter who's fucking, it's always kinda hot," I say.

"Depends."

"Don't pretend you're not rock hard."

You look me in the eye for two seconds, not answering, just breathing hard. Should you kiss me, tear my clothes off, take me then and there? You don't. You just say, "Okay, we should really look away. It's getting too embarrassing."

Still, we don't move.

"When I say go," you say. "One, two, three...go!"

You turn around, but I don't. Leaning against the railing, your back to the action, you take a pack of Craven A from your pocket, hand me a smoke, then light both our cigarettes.

"Of course, *you* didn't turn around," you say.

"Listen," I say, "if they're doing it out in the open, they

clearly want people to watch. I can literally not look anywhere else."

"You're horrible."

"If you really thought so, you wouldn't come home with me tonight."

You give me an intrigued look. "So we're hooking up?" you say.

"I already told you so."

"Just double-checking. When are we gonna kiss?"

"Not right away."

You hear a groan from down below. Then a metallic clinking sound, a belt being buckled up.

"FYI, the himbo just came," I say.

"That's the last thing I wanted to know, but thanks." You look me in the eye, take a long drag on your cig. "So what happens next?" you say.

YOU'LL TEXT SAM A SINGLE SENTENCE: "I JUST GOT dumped."

It'll be a beautiful day. The lilacs will be in bloom. Your neighbour will be out walking his puppy, a golden retriever, when you come out of your apartment. The air will feel light. It'll smell like summer that is just beginning and still full of promise.

But you, you'll be crying so hard you can't breathe.

Risking your life, you'll head off on your bike toward a bar where Sam's drinking on a patio with Max Lap and André. You've lost touch with reality, so you won't recognize the dangers in your surroundings. You'll nearly get hit by a bus when you run a red light, you'll almost get doored when you zip down a hill at top speed.

You'll be sorry you're spared because if you were sprawled out unconscious on the road with a leg torn off and blood coming out of your mouth, people would see you and rush to your rescue. Instead, you're suffering the worst pain of your life—no exaggeration, the worst by far, a ten out of ten—and you'll get zero sympathy. A dude crying his eyes out on the sidewalk at four in the afternoon evokes fear, not pity.

You'll imagine me finding out you were run over by a garbage truck. How I'd feel guilty and bad about myself. And that'll make you feel good inside. It'll warm your heart to imagine I regret breaking up with you.

But you won't get hit by a truck. You'll make it to the bar in one piece.

You'll step over the barrier that fences in the patio rather than go in through the entrance like a civilized human being, and you'll invade the space of people sitting nearby, without apologizing. ("I just got dumped," you'll inform them. "So I'm being an asshole today. Deal with it.") When you're finally seated with your friends, you'll find that your adrenaline rush has suddenly vanished and your muscles have turned to jelly. You'll sit slouched on a bench, staring at the ground. You can hardly speak. You'll just mutter answers to questions from André, Sam, and Max Lap that barely register in your brain.

You'll be forced to rally a bit when the waitress comes by.

"What can I get you?" she'll ask.

"What do you have for a guy who's just been dumped?"

She'll give you a sympathetic smile. "I've got you covered, sweetie," she'll say.

The guys will make awkward small talk, unable to find the right thing to say.

"Maybe it's for the best, bro," Sam will finally tell you.

"What the fuck are you talking about?" you'll reply.

"Did Laurie say she didn't love you anymore?"

"Yeah."

"Well, there you have it. You can't be with a girl who's fallen out of love. It's not an easy pill to swallow, I know, but it's pretty basic."

The waitress will come back with a tray in her hands. "I have a pint of my bitterest IPA," she'll say.

She'll set a coaster down gently in front of you. You'll wonder if she's showing you her cleavage on purpose or if your breakup has turned you into a sleazebag who sees come-ons everywhere.

"And I've also brought vodka pickles, on the house, to wash down the beer." She'll put down four shots, exactly two ounces each, perfectly prepared with a good vodka and the right-sized pickles.

Instead of thanking the poor girl, you'll just burst into tears.

THE EVENING WILL STRETCH OUT ENDLESSLY. MAX, ANDRÉ, and Sam will make sure you have a pint at least half full in front of you all through happy hour and that you never have to take out your wallet. The waitress will bring you all a few rounds of shots (three or four, you lose count) to make amends for making you cry. Gin, mescal, anything but vodka pickles to avoid setting you off again. The guys will manage to turn the incident into a joke and make the waitress laugh. You'll feel you have to laugh along to be part of the group. You'll realize that if we stubbornly force a smile, we can convince ourselves we feel good, even though the feeling lasts only a few seconds.

When it starts getting darker and cooler out, the guys will drag you a few blocks over to Le Terminal to see a show. At first, you'll refuse. "I don't think it's such a good idea," you'll say.

Max Lap will frown, unconvinced. "After breaking up with you, would Laurie go see a show at Le Terminal?" he'll say. "I don't think so."

"But if I'm going," you'll say, "why wouldn't she?"

"You're going because you have the *right* to be there," Sam will say. "And Laurie doesn't."

"No, she absolutely does not," you'll agree.

Sam will turn a bit more serious, lay a hand on your shoulder. "Listen," he'll say, "if she's there, we'll fuck off. Or better yet, we'll tell her to fuck off and it'll be entertaining."

That'll be persuasive enough for you to go through the door and up to the second floor of the club, but you can't chill out. As you wait for the lights to dim and the show to start, you'll keep a constant eye on the entrance in case I come up the stairs, stride across the room and come throttle you, tear you apart. At least two minutes will go by before you convince yourself I'd never arrive so late for a show. Your shoulders will loosen up a bit.

You'll finally manage to focus on the show but still feel pretty lousy. The third comic up will be a first-timer who's made his name on Instagram with some decent videos, but he won't be too comfortable onstage. He'll put a damper on the night because he has serious trouble interacting with his audience. His breathing will be strained, and his jokes, though pretty well-written, will fall flat. Out of habit, you'll turn to your right to share some withering comment with me, only to realize that no, it's true, I'm not there by your side and never will be again.

When you get up to go pee, at intermission, you'll find you're wobbly on your feet and Sam will notice even before you can say a word. He'll drag you to the green room to congratulate Arthur, a comedian who graduated from the comedy school a year after you. He was the opener that night, but you can't recall a single line from his set. Sam will sit you down in the green room, where the humid air will make you feel super nauseated. He'll take out a baggie of coke from the inside pocket of his bomber jacket and pour a little mound on the table, then cut it into three lines with his credit card. He'll roll up a twenty, hand it to you first. "At this rate, you're not gonna survive till eleven," he'll say. "So snort away."

You'll try replying with words, but only a groan will come out of your mouth. You'll vacuum up the line that Sam kindly prepared for you, and it'll be like a movie camera resetting its focus so the blur disappears. A moment of clarity. You can now follow what's going on around you and understand conversations again. Your nausea will be gone.

Sam will wave goodbye to Arthur, then pull you by the sleeve and lead you downstairs. He'll take a pack of smokes from his jacket, stick one in your mouth, light it. The nicotine will give you an extra layer of lucidity. You can't recall how much you've drunk, probably a lot, but you'll feel almost sober now.

Sam will look you in the eye, rub your shoulder. "You're fine, man. You're fine," he'll say. "Tell yourself that, okay?"

"Yeah."

"And fuck Laurie, okay?"

"I'm fine. And fuck Laurie."

"That's right, dude. Now say it with conviction."

Despite everything, you'll maybe feel a spark of joy, and it'll stir you, get you smiling. You'll clench your stomach, press hard on your diaphragm, and you'll shout so loud your voice echoes two blocks away: "I'm fine! And fuck Laurie! Fuck Laurie!"

Sam will burst out laughing, double over, come to lean on you to keep his balance. "You maniac! You see? I told you!"

You'll shout even louder: "I'm fine! And FUCK LAURIE!"

Two people nearby—girls your age or maybe even teens—will turn and give you the most disdainful look ever. Sam will crack up again. You'll realize that the therapeutic effect of your scream has already worn off, that you believed what you yelled for a moment there, but it couldn't last. But to humour Sam, you'll smile. You've never seen him like this, so good to you, so concerned, with no ulterior motive, no cutting remark to restore your power dynamic. You'll figure it maybe took something like this for Sam to show you he really cares, wants you to be happy, even though in today's world, it's good form to stab people in the back as proof that we're all fighting for a piece of the pie.

"Thanks, bro," you'll say.

"Don't mention it."

"I don't know what I'd do without you."

"Screw things up probably," he'll say. "Come here." He'll beckon you over, give you a big hug. As he pats your back, he'll whisper in your ear, "You're gonna be fine, I know it. I don't know how long it'll take, but you'll be fine."

Taking advantage of your moment of weakness, he'll slide his hands down your sides and, with a quick tug, pull your pants down and give you the hardest, strongest, sharpest slap on the ass you've ever had in your life. You can practically feel the shape of his hand burned into your skin while you stand there with your junk and butt exposed on Mount Royal Avenue. In the open window of a bus driving by, some old bat will give you an evil grin.

You'll bend over to pull your pants up and realize you're mooning everybody. You'll start to laugh hysterically. You'll double over, hands on your belly. You can't stop laughing. Practically choking, you'll pitch forward. Your forehead will hit the pavement, your knees on the ground, your ass in the air, your butthole on view for all to see. Long seconds will go by before you can control your breathing again and are coordinated enough to roll over, struggle to your feet, pull your pants up.

Sam will drag you back upstairs to your table just as the emcee returns to the stage to warm up the room for the second half, and you'll realize you've got a bit of gravel, or maybe even glass, embedded in your butt, and instead of hurting, it'll distract you. Any form of pain I didn't inflict is a welcome diversion.

YOU GUYS WILL SNEAK AWAY BEFORE THE SHOW ENDS, then drift over to the West Shefford without anyone actually suggesting it. Sam will let Max Lap and André lead the way, but then he'll drag you into a corner store on Mount Royal Avenue.

The place will smell like overripe bananas, a wet dog, and stale beer drying in empties returned for a deposit. The neon will burn your retinas, contrasting with the relative darkness you've been immersed in most of the night.

Sam will go to the checkout counter. "A pack of Bensons twenty-five," he'll say.

The clerk at the cash will be about your age, also short, unsmiling, and practically invisible. He'll turn to the shelf behind him, lift the metal flap, take out a pack, lay it on the counter over the spread of lottery tickets.

Sam will look the dude in the eye for two seconds, very serious. In a flat tone you've never previously heard him use, he'll murmur this: "I've bought matches here before."

The clerk will glance toward the front door, then press a button under the counter. You'll hear the door lock. When he lifts his hand from beneath the counter, his fist will be closed. Sam will hand him a one-hundred-dollar bill. The clerk will open his fist over Sam's hand and drop a small baggie of coke into it. He'll press the button under the counter again, and the front door will unlock.

In a completely natural voice, the clerk will say, "That'll be fifteen twenty-five."

"Credit," Sam will say.

Sam will tap his card on the reader, take his pack of smokes.

"Thanks a lot," he'll say, looking the dude in the eye.

"Have a good night," the clerk will answer right back.

Outside, Sam will drag you into an alley and behind a dumpster. "It's fucking overpriced and probably cut with ground glass," he'll say, opening the baggie in front of you. "But as a last resort, it does the trick."

You'll fill the end of your car key with the coke, then snort it with one nostril. It'll be cold, abrasive, and go down your throat leaving behind a taste of Tylenol. You'll immediately feel different—sharper, better looking, more agile. Your hearing will be keener. The cars in the street at the other end of the block, two girls chatting and laughing on the sidewalk, the buzz of the street light above you—everything will be clearer.

You'll arrive in time to catch the last comic, Jérémie, a nice guy but a bit of a hack. He'll be hard to watch, but the audience will applaud out of pity. Sam will be approached by some girl who seems more like a fan than a friend, given how often she laughs (every time Sam finishes a sentence, which makes you want to pour your beer over her elaborate hairdo).

The club will be full, and everything will be complicated: getting to the bathroom, ordering a beer, finding the guys in the crowd. You'll be forced to focus on the essentials: alcohol, coke, pissing.

You'll make it to last call without having even one coherent conversation. The best you can do will be to exchange smiles, nod your head, fake it that you hear what someone's saying to you. You'll muddle through with only two or three mishaps when people figure out you're just smiling stupidly and pretending to listen. Meanwhile, Sam will be busy chatting up the girl who's latched onto your group. André and Max Lap have long given up talking to you, but they'll be civil enough to buy you shots now and then and give you a thumbs-up or a pat on the back to show that yes, they do like you, but that you're a bit too high maintenance at the moment. Apart from that, you'll pass the time by listening to a girl you dated for two weeks in cégep, an actor you played hockey with twice, and a dude you did improv with in high school.

When you come out of the bathroom for the eleventh time that night, Max Lap will signal you to follow him. "We're going back to my place," he'll say.

And just as he finishes his sentence, you'll see a taxi van pull up out of nowhere and a heartbeat later you'll catch the girl with the dyed hair by the arm after she slips on the staircase going up to Max Lap's place and practically falls into you. "Look, we don't even *know* you," you'll bark at her. "So don't ruin our night by falling down the stairs and forcing us to take you to emergency, okay?"

She'll back away, clearly afraid of you. You'll let out a laugh to defuse the situation, but she'll still look uneasy. Ahead of you, Max Lap and André will also laugh to show it was all a joke. But it wasn't really. You won't be in the mood to make conversation with Sam's groupie, but Sam's in seduction mode, so you have to put up with her.

Max Lap's apartment will smell like weed and cat litter. The walls will be white with nothing on them—no posters, no paintings, zip. There'll be four hockey sticks leaning together in the entranceway, pizza boxes stacked on the coffee table in the living room, empty beer cans left on the dining-room table. He's kept his laptop open, probably to show any visitors that he's working hard to become a respectable comedian.

He'll push his laptop aside, throw the beer cans in the trash, look in the fridge. Then he'll open a cupboard and come back to the table with three Pabsts, a quarter bottle of Johnnie Walker, and the last swigs of a Jack Daniel's. "It's not much, but it's what I've got," he'll say.

"Beggars can't be choosers," André will say.

Sam will lay his baggie of coke on the table. There'll be just a thin line about two millimetres thick at the bottom. "Anyone got any blow?" he'll ask.

"Fuck, I literally wish I did," the girl will say.

You and Max Lap will stare at her blankly awhile so she knows that everything that comes out of her mouth is super annoying.

"I've got nothing," Max Lap will say.

"That's okay," Sam will say, taking his phone from his pocket. "I've got a little left...and I have a phone number."

You and the other guys won't have a phone number, so you feel kinda inferior. Not having a dealer turns you into a leech, makes you dependent on somebody else who has an in. Push that logic further, not having a phone number means you have no street cred, that you aren't savvy enough to zero in on the person at the party who can get you VIP access. Not having a number means you're not cool. Sam, though, he's cool. He likes to remind you of that. You've asked him for his dealer's number a few times, and each time he said sure, he'd give it to you, but then he never did, and you didn't want to push too hard in case you looked even more pathetic by begging.

Forty minutes later, when you're down to scraping the bottom of the baggie with a little spoon to pick up any microscopic particles of coke and rubbing your gums with the residue till you bleed, the doorbell will ring. When Sam gets up, you'll follow him and whisper, "Can you ask him if I can have his number? I think I'm gonna need it."

Sam will nod with a complicit grin, and you'll go sit back down with Max Lap and André, who are dissecting each gag from Jérémie's set earlier. André will jot down notes so he can send them to Jérémie the next day. Did Jérémie ask you guys for notes? No, and he isn't even really a friend of yours, he's an acquaintance at best, but you'll all be too high to realize that.

Your cell will vibrate—Sam sending you a phone number with no other text. He'll bound back upstairs right after and drop a much bigger baggie on the table. "We're good to go, boys," he'll say reassuringly.

He'll give you a discreet smile as if to say, "You're welcome," then cut lines on the table with the precision of a sushi chef. Sam's ADHD sometimes expresses itself in weird ways: at school, he had a tough time following any lecture over thirty minutes long, but he can waste two hours grouping apps on his phone by colour; he can forget three appointments because he's busy cleaning his apartment; he can be hyperfocused and block out all conversation around him while doing something as trivial as cutting four lines of coke.

Watching Sam, Max Lap will say to you, "So whatcha gonna do about your show?"

Sam will look up from the table. "Let's not talk about that," he'll say. "The poor guy has had enough for one day."

"No, it's okay," you'll say. "The dust has settled."

"It's been six hours," Sam will say. "The dust has *not* settled."

"I'm having a good time tonight. I feel better."

Sam will nod.

"We talked about it," you'll say. "We don't think it'd be a good idea to stop collaborating, especially with the premiere five months away. I mean, we just started the previews, so we aren't gonna rewrite the whole show."

You won't have the balls to admit you told me you never wanted to work with me again. You pleaded with me in fact.

"You have no problem with that?" André will ask.

"No, no, we're both adults. And it'd be a big loss if we didn't keep working together. We have nothing to gain by stopping."

"That's cool if you manage to keep a good working relationship," André will say.

"I don't think so," Sam will say. "No, you gotta cut ties. You can't let your career depend on Laurie, bro. This is your big break. Don't let her steal it away."

Before you can answer, the girl will cry, "Did your girlfriend break up with you?"

"Yeah."

"When exactly?"

"Well, about six hours ago, like Sam said."

"Oh, how you handling it?" she'll ask shrilly.

You'll hesitate, then say, "I dunno, I—"

"Were you together long?"

"Like two years."

"If I was you, I'd be literally devastated."

"If you want, I can slash my fucking wrists right here, right now."

The guys will laugh, but the girl won't find it so funny.

"Don't scare her off," Sam will say. "I plan on sleeping with her."

This will draw a smile from Max Lap. The girl will lower her eyes.

Sam will take a twenty out of his wallet. "It's ready, guys," he'll say.

THE SUN HAS ALREADY BEEN UP FOR OVER TWO HOURS when your phone rings. You guys sent the girl to the corner store as soon as the beer fridges were unlocked at eight a.m., and you'll now be sipping a cool Pabst and grinding your teeth.

There'll be maybe a quarter baggie of the coke left. Sam will be smoking a joint under the range hood while the girl leans against the kitchen counter in front of him and clenches her jaw tight enough to wear the enamel off her teeth. She'll try jumping into the conversation but can barely get a word in because Max Lap will rattle on about his plan to set up an alternative comedy festival that will showcase edgier, less mainstream material without worrying about marketability. You'll cut in excitedly every now and then with "Yes!" and "Totally!" Your brain has been fried for at least three hours, but despite that you'll keep on snorting because you'll notice that whenever the coke's effect wears off, you'll start staring into space or at some corner of Max Lap's dingy apartment, then you'll drift out of your body and picture me at that moment—what I'm doing, where I am, who I'm with, how I feel. The answer will be pretty clear each time. I'm probably slowly waking up, relaxed, rested, freed from the burden of having to break up with my annoying boyfriend, and when you picture this, your eyes will well up, so you'll lean over the table to take another bump and the feeling will pass. For a few minutes, it'll pass. Taking a hit will let you feel briefly in control again, remind you that I'm basically a stupid bitch who has no idea what I've let go and that the next time I see you onstage, it'll become crystal clear to me the huge mistake I've made.

After you snort another line, you'll see that Thomas is calling you.

"Raph?" he'll say, overly cheerful. "Where are you?"

"Um...at Max's. Why?"

"Max? Max who?"

"Max Lap."

"At eight twenty in the morning?"

"Oh, is it that late already?"

"The radio station just called. They asked if you're on your way. You're supposed to be on air in ten minutes."

You'll instantly come down from your high.

"Fuck. I won't make it."

"Is your radio piece ready?"

You sent in your topic on Friday before heading off for the weekend, but you haven't exactly been in the mood to work on it.

"Yeah, of course it is. I just needed, like, to drop something off at Max's. But the traffic—"

"You won't arrive in time, I guess?"

"I...no, I won't."

You'll motion to Max Lap to cut the music. You'll move away from the table, look out the window. In the street, a garbageman will be putting on an Olympic performance by throwing trash bags into a moving garbage truck, then jogging to catch up to it. A dude in a suit, phone to his ear, will get into an Audi while a hooker gives him the eye.

A feeling of imminent death.

"Want me to cancel? Or would you rather do it by phone?"

You'll picture me making breakfast alone in my kitchen,

my coffee steaming on the counter as I listen distractedly to the radio. You'll picture me raising an eyebrow when I hear the host fumbling as he realizes he now has six extra minutes of content to fill. You'll picture me thinking that's it, I've crushed you, that you're weak and unable to deal with the slightest obstacle that life, or your ex, throws your way.

"I'll, um, I'll do it. By phone. If it's alright with them."

"I'll call them back, then text you if it's a go, okay?"

"Okay."

"Don't do this too often. I don't think they're overjoyed in the control room right now."

"No, no, course not. You know what it's like, the damn traffic."

"Yeah, yeah, okay. I'll be in touch."

You'll hang up, then turn to the guys and, especially, to the girl. "I need you all to shut up for six minutes," you'll say. "I'm in deep shit."

"SO, RAPH, YOU WANTED TO GIVE US SOME TIPS ON planning a vacation, right?"

The radio producer was as dry as toast with you when she answered your call. As a greeting, she just said, "Okay, I'll patch you through to the studio." Then the technician just said, "It sounds like you're in your bathroom. Can you change locations?"

You came out of Max Lap's bathroom and asked everyone to go smoke outside for a few minutes so you could use the living room to get better sound.

"Yeah, well, I went away for a weekend with friends and figured it might be a good idea to share my experience so I can help your listeners avoid embarrassing situations. Because that's basically my role here—to get myself into these messes so other people don't make the same mistakes. We're a public-service program."

"So where do we start, Raph?"

"First thing I suggest is always have an escape plan. Vacations are fun, but they can quickly turn into a nightmare. You head off camping with your best bud, then discover he likes spooning in his sleep and keeps mistaking you for his body pillow. Escape plan!"

Laughter on the crackly phone line. "So what exactly is this escape plan?" the host will ask.

"Well, all the classics are good. You left a burner on, forgot an appointment, found a weird lump on your body. You discover you have an illegitimate child. Anything, as long as you have a way out."

"Okay, got it. So suppose your vacation goes to hell and you need to use your excuse to escape. How do you go about it? Because you can't get out of every situation."

"Well, the thing is you gotta plan ahead. Ideally, you need a fast and easy way to get back home. Say you go on a road trip with friends. Well, make sure you take your own car."

"Now that's not a bad idea."

"Another thing: limit your trip to a distance that lets you return home fast. If you're just a stone's throw from your place, it's easier to get home when your travelling companion—and former friend—starts to breathe in the fresh air and micromanage your snacks. It's never fun to discover your best bud turns into the lady from *Eat Pray Love* once he's on holiday. Another tip: limit your risks. For example, avoid travelling with other people and you'll run much less risk of getting into a jam. And why not stick with low-risk activities, like watching TV, playing Scrabble, or just thinking about sports you like. That way, you'll also avoid nasty surprises, like finding yourself on some island with ferry service only once a day and getting stuck there with no way out when your girlfriend dumps you and you start combing the beach for rusty nails to jab into your throat so you'll die of a severe case of tetanus before the next ferry comes."

On the other end of the line, the whole studio will burst out laughing.

"So really, instead of a group road trip, just stay home, avoid other humans, and check out Netflix. If you really wanna go wild, put on 'Life Is a Highway' when you get up to pee."

"Thanks for those excellent tips, Raph. With your help, I'm sure we can now travel far and wide and enjoy all kinds of new experiences. I don't know what we'd do without you."

I don't know what we'd do without you.

Sometimes, you'll hear a phrase and twist its meaning so it applies to me. It'll be a real gut punch. The confidence you've gained by snorting coke all night and doing a pretty decent radio feature with no preparation whatsoever will dissolve in an instant when, in your head, you hear *I don't know what I'd do without you.* You'll have no idea what you'll do without me. You won't even know how you'll make it through the day.

But none of that will be apparent on air. The host has already moved on to the next topic, and the producer will be back on the line with you, upbeat now, like she's totally forgotten you almost fucked up her show.

"You were awesome, Raph. Always a pleasure."

"Talk next week."

Right after she hangs up, your phone will ring.

"Shit, you really scared me." It'll be Thomas. "But you killed as always. Real sharp. God are you ever good on the radio."

"They aren't pissed at me?"

"As long as you give them their six minutes of content and everyone in the studio laughs, you can be a total prick, dude, and everything will still be fine. It's the untalented who can't afford to be jerks. You, you could be Jeffrey Dahmer and everyone would forgive you."

"Was I funny?"

"Hilarious. The part about your girlfriend leaving you, I laughed. Imagine if it happened."

"Are you fucking serious, Thomas?"

"What?"

"Where were you all weekend?"

"Huh?"

"You didn't notice anything off?"

"Well, no. I mean..." A pause on the line. "You're serious? Laurie broke up with you?"

You'll have to lean against the counter because it's like a thirty-foot wave is bearing down on you again. Your lower lip will tremble, your eyes will tear up. A bayonet will stab you in the belly.

"I'm gonna die, Thomas. I'm gonna fucking die."

"No, no, don't freak, okay? We'll take this one step at a time. I'll cancel your appointments today. I'll come get you and we'll figure out a game plan, okay?"

NO MATTER HOW MANY GAME PLANS THOMAS COMES up with, there'll be no saving you, at least not at first. Yes, he'll do whatever it takes to make you feel important: take you to a spa, pay for a massage (you'll cut it short to go puke since you drank an incredible amount of alcohol but barely felt it on account of all the coke), and postpone your gig the next day, claiming previews can be moved around. The next night, you'll realize that vegging at home in front of Netflix while downing a twelve-pack is no way to cheer yourself up, so you'll instruct Thomas not to cancel any more gigs and, if he can, to even book you a few nights in clubs so you can keep testing out your material, even though your preview run's already under way, because you want to test, test, test, and test some more and, ideally, not spend a single night at home alone.

And when you do have a night off, you'll go see friends at some comedy club, boozing it up the minute you walk through the door. The weeks will be one long, painful day you spend either hammered or hungover, but thinking of me almost constantly and wondering where I might be, what I might be doing, who I might be with since I'm not with you. You won't call, write, or even try to run into me, but I'll never be as present in your life. All your days will be spent thinking of me, only me.

You won't hold out hope I'll come back to you, not really. You knew what you were getting into. The breakup, even though you wish it never happened, won't surprise you. You never had a chance in hell, since you knew I was out of your league.

You'll start sleeping around—just because. Max Lap will introduce you to a friend of his one night after one of your gigs. She'll be pretty and funny and even a nice person. Her name will be Karine or Évelyne or Marine, something like that, and Max Lap will whisper to you that she just got dumped too, so you'll naturally be drawn to each other, like black holes trying to swallow each other's void. You'll go home together, and while you're fucking—awkwardly because you aren't used to having sex with women other than me—you'll say, "I don't know how anybody could've left you."

I don't know how anybody could've left you.

Even though she's really lovely and the sex is totally fine under the circumstances, what you say won't be true. You'll obviously know how somebody could've left her. You understand how a person can leave another person. People leave each other all the time. What you're really telling her, that poor girl who's just minding her own business, is that you don't know how I could've left *you*.

You'll know why deep down, though. You've known since you first came over to chat me up earlier. From the start, you've needed me way too much for our story to end well.

YOU'LL HAVE A RECURRING NIGHTMARE. YOU WAKE UP
all alone on an island. The sky's orange, almost red, a kind
of twilight or dawn, almost artificial, like the light pollution
from distant greenhouses. You don't know why, but you're
sure you're late and need to hurry to the dock to catch a ferry.
You arrive just as the ferry pulls away, and you see I'm on the
boat, my back to you. You shout my name, but I don't turn
around.

When you wake up, you'll be so relieved you were only
dreaming. Two seconds later, you'll remember that, in fact, I
have left you, that you're all alone.

Those two seconds when you think that nightmare scenario never happened will be the best seconds of your day.
The rest of the time, you'll be haunted by me.

You'll pray that someone somewhere convinces you that
someday you'll stop waking up like that.

You'll feel better someday, I swear to you. But by this point,
you've forgotten what I said.

One thing that helps you cope—though it doesn't really
make you feel any better—will be to call me a cunt. It'll
become a catchphrase. You'll be having a drink before a gig,
or after a gig, or at a party, or during last call, and you'll let
your guard down and forget Sam's golden rule that the name
"Laurie" must never cross your lips. For example:

Sam: "I'm going to Iceland next summer."

You: "Iceland? Cool. Laurie went there once and—"

Sam: "Raaaph..."

The golden rule will come back to you. You'll be forced, whenever you say my name, to follow up with this: "Laurie's a cunt."

Then everyone will repeat together, "Laurie's a cunt," in a monotone.

But your friends will be flexible on this point, and if you start carrying on and on about me, they might just nod in agreement and even fan the flames, so you'll end up believing you're in the right given that you're the one in pain.

You won't see the truth since you never really try to see my side of the story. One time, Thomas will say, "Maybe you don't need to start a war with Laurie, though."

"What the fuck do you know?" you'll tell him. "She wasn't *your* girlfriend, was she?"

Thomas won't know what to say to that. He'll never mention me to you again. No one else will try to portray me as anything but the Antichrist.

But if you wanted to hear the truth, you'd learn I wasn't put on this earth to destroy you. The truth is I'll think about you way less than you will about me.

It'd be worse to find that out. Worse to know I'm just not that interested in you. You'd rather that I love you, but if I can't, then you'd settle for me hating you. But indifference? No, that's just not acceptable.

Hating somebody is one way of keeping them close.

WHEN YOU GO BACK TO GATINEAU TO DO ANOTHER preview, Thomas will go along and won't leave your side in case you suddenly drop dead. Your producer will book you a different hotel that's not as nice or as comfortable, but it's the only option for you because just the sight of the place where you stayed the last time will be enough to get your heart hammering in your chest for a good half-hour.

You'll often react this way to places we went to together. You'll take different routes just to forget these places exist. To forget I exist.

You'll go for a drink with Max Lap after the gig and run into that Radio-Canada reporter who interviewed you— Audrey. She'll end up sitting down with you guys. You won't know if you should keep a professional distance, but she'll be chill, not like on the job, not as stiff. She'll be cool and funny. It'll be a nice night. She'll go back to the hotel with you.

You'll have to go to Ottawa, Gatineau, and Abitibi a few times in the following weeks, so you'll stop in to see her because, unlike a lot of girls, it won't impress her much that your name's Raph Massi.

You'll like her a lot because you soon realize she's as sad as you are. Maybe even sadder. It'll reassure you to know you haven't hit rock bottom. But it'll scare you to realize you could fall even farther.

She'll be mourning her father, who died recently, but she'll tell you that's not the real issue, that she's been like this for ages, that she was sad long before for no particular reason.

"I'm pretty used to feeling miserable," she'll say. "So it's no big deal."

"You didn't look miserable the first time I met you," you'll say. "To me, you looked radiant."

"You know how you look?" she'll say.

"No."

"Too shallow to be feeling sad."

That'll make you smile. "I'll take that as a compliment," you'll say.

The nights you spend together, you'll mostly just smoke weed, drink beer, and fuck (yeah, the sex will be good, in case you're wondering, not better than with me, no, but just as good, though different too). Your relationship won't be much, but it'll be what you need.

One time, after you fuck, you'll share a joint while sitting up in bed and listening to music and you'll ask, "You hooking up with anyone besides me?"

"No one on the regular," she'll tell you. "I've watched my mom since my dad died, and I think, fuck, I can't depend on just one person to the point where it'd kill me if I lost them."

You'll take a big drag on your joint, then exhale slowly and stare at the ceiling. A lump will form in your throat. You'll be scared to swallow, scared the slightest movement will betray how sad you are that you totally, completely, irrevocably agree with what she just said.

Through pursed lips, you'll say, "I feel you."

"It's better to be alone," she'll say, matter-of-fact, "and just focus on friends. My friends are reliable at least. And I can have twenty of them at the same time."

You can see right through her when she's sad and pretends everything's fine, even though everything's fucked. But this time you won't feel she's bullshitting. After confiding this, she'll suddenly seem lighter and freer. You'll wonder if, despite your best intentions, you might end up alone for the rest of your life. This will make you want to sink into a hole and disappear from the world without a sound.

In July, your mom will call you one evening while you're with Audrey.

"Raphaël?"

"Yeah."

Audrey will frown as soon as you speak.

"How are things?" your mom will ask.

"Things are good," you'll say, stealing the lit spliff out of Audrey's hand. "Things are good."

"I ran into Maryse at the grocery store. She said she never misses you on the radio."

"Oh, that's great."

You'll suck on the joint. Exhale slowly, your mouth wide.

"Hey, I thought you were really funny on *Le Tricheur* the other day."

"Yeah, game shows are always fun to do."

"How's the test run going for your show?"

"Oh, it's going good, really good."

"I can't wait to see it."

"Yeah, same."

There'll be a moment of silence on the line. Then your mom will say, "Is everything okay?"

"Uh-huh."

"You getting some exercise?"

"Jeez..."

"It's good for your mental health, y'know."

You'll choke up a bit, unable to reveal anything further, although you've already told her about the breakup.

There'll be another moment of silence, then your mom

will take a breath that's a bit taut and trembly. "I've got some bad news," she'll finally say. "Grandma died."

You won't know how to react. You'll feel Audrey's eyes on you, wondering what's going on.

You'll stick to the facts: "When?"

"Yesterday. A stroke."

"What time?"

"In the afternoon."

"What happened?"

"Well, her neighbour called the ambulance. Grandma was lying on the ground in her yard. Face down."

You won't know what else to ask. You'll be glad your mom waited before sharing the news. You couldn't have handled it in the frenzy of the first twenty-four hours.

"The service is this weekend in L'Ancienne-Lorette. I know it's complicated for you with your tour..."

"Yeah, it is. I've got gigs this weekend."

"Well, I don't want you feeling guilty. I guess you can't cancel a show?"

"No."

You'll flash back to when you were curled up in a ball in front of your hotel-room door in Gatineau. That feeling you had—like your internal organs had been set on fire.

"Well then, Grandma wouldn't have wanted you to cancel. So, look, why don't we FaceTime from the reception. You can say hello to everyone that way."

"That would work."

"I wouldn't want to keep you from your fans."

"My fans would get over it, I'm sure."

"No, I'm saying that for *you*. I'm happy that people like you now."

You'll flash back to high school. You're in your gym clothes, hair sopping wet, a dank smell clinging to your skin. You're seated in the principal's office waiting for your mom to come get you after some kids dumped a bucket of mop water over your head in front of the lockers.

Your mom will be happy that people finally like you. "I have to let you go," she'll say. "We'll talk on Saturday."

You'll hang up. Audrey will stare at you, a bit more concerned now. "That was a weird call," she'll say. "Who was it?"

"My mom. My grandma just died."

Audrey will hug you close. "Oh, god, I'm sorry," she'll say. "I'm *so* sorry."

"But I don't feel anything."

"Nothing?"

"Nothing."

"You didn't like your grandmother?"

"No, I liked her a lot, but, like, it's not a huge shock. She was old. Old people do die."

Audrey will draw back to look at you, unsure, wondering if you're kidding. "When my dad died, I was devastated," she'll say. "I didn't sleep for a week. I couldn't eat, couldn't work. I was a zombie."

"I felt worse when I got dumped, I think."

She'll look at you like she's just come face to face with a home invader.

"Am I a bad person?" you'll say blankly.

"Have you always been like this?"

"Like what?"

The two of you will never hook up again.

AFTER TWO MONTHS WITHOUT SLEEP, YOU'LL GO TO A WALK-in clinic for a prescription for sleeping pills.

The doctor will ask too many questions, like "How much alcohol do you drink a week?"

"I dunno," you'll say. "About three to five beers a day, I guess."

She'll turn all serious, pause a bit, then say, "If I suggested you go to rehab, what would you say?"

"I'm a stand-up comedian, doctor. Drinking's part of my job."

YOU NEVER LIKE GOING TO QUEBEC CITY, SO YOU WON'T
be too eager to preview your show there.

Still, the Grand Théâtre is a great venue—comfortable,
excellent facilities, nice staff. Daniel will book you a room at
Château Frontenac, and there are good restaurants nearby
for a late meal after a gig. The problem, though, is you'll feel
you've regressed ten years as soon as you cross Pierre Laporte
Bridge.

When you got into the comedy school and left for
Montreal a few years back, you felt you could reinvent yourself and choose who exactly you were for the first time in your
life. Whenever you go back to Quebec City, the new you gets
entirely erased. You always wind up running into someone
you know. And suddenly you become a fourteen-year-old
kid again, slinking around his school, getting spit on and
called a faggot, getting food thrown at him in the cafeteria,
all because...because why exactly?

You hate Sam's obsession with high school because onstage
you aren't able to tell a single story about your time at school.
You're basically envious. Even though you realize your life
would probably be way less interesting if you'd been one of
the cool kids. Your career's your revenge.

After your gigs, you'll always stick around a half-hour,
sometimes even an hour, to greet your fans and pose for selfies. Teenage girls will stand there blushing as they struggle
to find something to say to you. Ladies in their forties might
grab your butt as their husbands snap a photo of them with

you. You'll be good at these interactions. You'll find ways to get people talking, make them feel important. Even though as individuals they bore you, you'll understand you need to treat your fans well.

In our field, this is super important. All other relationships become complicated: your fellow comics envy you in an unhealthy way, your family never truly understands you, your friends drift away, but your fans, if you're good to them, they're good to you. That's why you have to give them what they want all the time. Even if it costs you. Even if it drains you.

There'll be a girl your age waiting to talk to you in the lobby. "Raph, you were amazing," she'll say. She'll be way more casual with you than the average fan.

"Oh, thanks a lot. Was this your first time seeing my act?"

"Well, I did see you do improv back in high school."

You won't recognize her, which she finally realizes. "Don't know if you remember me," she'll say. "I'm Vicky."

"Vicky?"

"Vicky Chénier."

You'll vaguely recall who she is. She used to date some hockey player who got off on slamming you against the wall whenever he spotted you in the school hallway.

"Oh yeah, Vicky, of course. Sorry about that."

"I changed my hairstyle, that's why."

Her hair will look like any girl's hair, but you'll lie: "Yes, it's the hair."

"Anyway, it was so great seeing you onstage. The show's awesome. Your career's really taken off. I always get a kick out of seeing you on TV."

The crowd will thin out till nobody's left in the lobby but you, Vicky, and an usher closing up.

"Yeah, I've been super lucky," you'll say. "What are you up to nowadays?"

"Oh, me, I'm a dental hygienist, in Sainte-Foy. It's been three years now."

"Cool."

"It's a fun job."

There'll be a slight pause. She'll fidget, shuffle her feet, then look you in the eye. "Got any plans tonight?" she'll ask.

"ARE YOU SINGLE?"

You'll mutter a nonchalant uh-huh as you lie naked and sweaty in bed watching Vicky get dressed. You're scared that if you say anything more, you'll betray a weakness and that the tone of your voice, a hesitation, a poorly chosen word will scream this: *Yeah, I'm single, it's been three months, I'm still not over my ex, I cry a lot, I cry all the time, I think about her non-stop.* You're scared Vicky will hear all that and you'll lose your sway over her.

She'll fasten her bra, her back to you. Watching her, you'll realize how pretty she is. A beautiful girl way out of your league.

"Yeah, I guess with your career," she'll mutter, "you don't have much time for a girlfriend."

"True. What about you? If you're asking that question, you're probably sneaking around behind someone's back."

She'll turn around, pull up her skinny jeans, let out a little mischievous laugh, both sheepish and carefree. "Shh!" she'll say. Then: "Yeah, I'm still with Jonathan."

"Jonathan?"

"Jonathan Théorêt. My boyfriend since grade ten."

"Oh, yeah, Jonathan Théorêt."

Jonathan Théorêt. The hockey bro. The handsome dude who tipped over the porta-potty you were peeing in during a field trip. Jonathan fucking Théorêt.

"Yep. But, uh, Jo is working on hydro projects up north. He's in La Romaine right now. So, well, you know how it is.

He's gone a long time."

"Hmm."

She'll go to the window, glance down. Your room will overlook a courtyard. "It's lovely here, isn't it?" she'll say. "Can you believe I've never spent a night at Château Frontenac?"

Yes, you can believe it.

"When you live in Quebec City," she'll say, "renting a room here somehow seems less appealing."

"Yeah."

"You don't stay with your parents when you're in town?"

"Oh, you know how it is. I finish late, and they have their own routine."

She'll bend down, pick up her T-shirt, slip it on. "It was great catching up," she'll say. "I'd stay, but, well, you know..."

"Yeah."

"It's cool to see how far you've come. I mean, it was clear to everyone you'd go far. I'm really happy for you."

"It was clear to everyone I'd go far?"

"It sure was."

"People thought that?"

"Well...yeah, they did."

"Did your boyfriend?"

She'll tense up a bit. "Uh, yeah, I think so," she'll say. "Jo's a big fan of your work too."

You'll sit up in bed, still naked, your dick still wet. There'll be a half second when you figure you can keep your mouth shut, that you don't need to respond, that you can just let Vicky leave, that she can go home satisfied she's done something naughty and gotten away with it.

You'll have a chance not to stir up trouble. Instead, you'll deliberately choose to look Vicky in the face, squint your eyes, clench your fists, then say, "Was Jo a fan before or after he covered me in shit? Before or after he swiped my clothes while I was in the shower? Before or after he bound me with duct tape and left me in the big sink in the bathroom?"

Vicky will let out a nervous laugh, like she thinks you're just joking. She'll pause a second, uncomfortable, then say, "I think you're exaggerating, Raph. I mean, I'm sorry you got picked on at school, I really am sorry, but sometimes, you know how it is, we remember things worse than they were."

"I don't really give a fuck, Vicky. Everybody's got some sob story about high school. I'm not traumatized for life. But don't go saying you all respected me, because it's not true. Everyone treated me like a freaking turd for five years. And it's fine, it's okay. But don't pretend otherwise, just because you all suddenly like what I do and wanna brag you knew me before I hit it big."

She'll put her hand on the doorknob. "I'm gonna go," she'll say.

"Anyway, I don't give two shits. There's an advantage to being unpopular in high school. Jonathan Théorêt might've done some awful stuff to me, but at least he never fucked my girlfriend."

You'll rarely hear a door slam so hard.

You'll feel good afterward. It won't last more than a minute, but you'll feel good.

CLAIRE WILL POST A STORY SHOWING HER TICKET TO YOUR premiere. Next to her in the photo will be a knee covered by a sundress. My sundress, you'll know, because two weeks earlier you saw me wearing it in a Facebook photo of my road trip to Gaspésie.

Claire's the girl I was talking to tonight, my friend who made you think I was queer.

Claire could only have gotten a ticket through me. She'll be my plus-one, meaning I'll be there on opening night, even though I stopped working on the show five months earlier when you and me split.

You aren't anxious by nature. Anxious people are worried about the future, and it's everything that might eventually go wrong that terrifies them. Your problem's not the future, but the past. Your mind's kept pretty busy looping through past fuck-ups: the time you got caught jerking off in the school bathroom, the time you spent a half-hour badmouthing the latest show by the comedian Guillaume Wagner only to realize his manager was sitting at your table, the time you got arrested for shoplifting at Rossy, the time you peed your pants in class, the time you sneezed on the actor Anne-Élisabeth Bossé at the Gémeaux Awards, the time you got so tanked you staggered into the wrong apartment and woke up in your neighbour's bed. There are so many gaffes like this—moments when you were just *too much* and at the worst possible time—that you could replay them in a loop forever and never get bored. You're a masochist, and that's why you're so successful. Normal people fill photo albums with happy memories, whereas your memories just torment you and make you hate yourself a little more. This forces you to look for love any way you can. Your career would never end up taking off if you liked yourself.

But the night of your Montreal premiere, things will be different. Because the Pope himself could be in the house and you wouldn't give a shit. Probably you'd single him out, roast the dude, make quips about pedophilia since pervert-priest jokes, though they're pretty trite, always kill. Why do tens of thousands of people, hundreds of thousands even, click on your videos? Why do fans pay to see your act? Because you've got a big mouth the average Joe can't allow himself. Most of us learn early in life that to succeed, we have to keep our traps shut and toe the line. Your life inspires your fans because it sells the idea of freedom.

Anyway, the Pope won't be in the audience, but some big-wigs in the church of comedy will be: bookers who you'll count on to organize a tour with a slew of dates; critics who, fingers crossed, won't be pricks and write total bullshit; and managers and comedians who'll hate on you and hopefully skewer the show as they drink the free cheap wine after your performance, a sign they envy you so much they're scared of you and feel the need to crap on you to save face.

Those people will be in the house, and you won't give a fuck, even though technically they have the power of life and death over your work. Claire will be there too. And undoubtedly, beside her, will be me, which you just can't accept.

It'll be seven thirty-two. The stage manager will come by the green room two minutes late to give you your thirty-minute call, and Thomas will show up just behind her in his snazzy premiere outfit—dress pants, a V-neck T-shirt, a blazer. "The man!" he'll cry.

You'll stay slumped in your chair, feet up on the counter, the mirror in front of you showing your reflection—a corpse with a nice tan since you made sure to apply enough makeup to look alive. You won't have the energy to stand up. You'll just turn your head a bit toward Thomas. To do more would take too much effort.

Thomas will come up behind you and massage your shoulders vigorously. "Ready to kick some ass?" he'll say.

Your voice will be flat and subdued. "I guess the team wouldn't let me go onstage if I wasn't totally ready, so..."

"Of course we wouldn't."

"Unless it's too much trouble rescheduling the tour and everyone's just like, 'Well, fuck, we'll just let him go on and whatever happens happens.'"

"That's crazy talk," Thomas will say.

"I know. Just joking."

"I assure you the show's fantastic. Daniel is super excited."

Thomas always tells you you're good, he'll always tell you you're good. It's reassuring, but eventually you won't really trust his judgment. You could take a dump onstage, and he'd probably tell you that you're breaking new ground. It's an occupational hazard. A category-five hurricane could hit Montreal and the typical manager would assure you that it's great news, that it's all good, that he's really optimistic about the future, and that he caught your performance last night and you were excellent, really, at your best, but he'll have to phone you back because he has another call.

"You must be excited," Thomas will say.

"Yeah."

It's not that you'll want to worry him, but it'll be too hard for you to pretend to be happy to be there. The only thing you'll see whenever you close your eyes is an empty theatre with me sitting in the middle, in the best seat in the house, watching you, arms crossed, ready to despise you.

"Tonight's quite the accomplishment. This is a turning point, bud. Starting tomorrow morning, things are gonna be totally different."

"Come on, Thom, things don't really work that way."

"Well, they do and they don't. You're already sold out till Christmas, you know."

"I know, I know."

"I'm telling you, the show's terrific. People are gonna love it. People already love it."

Thomas's lack of intelligence is often a good quality. Since he fails to see the big picture and grasp all the subtleties of a situation, he can be, or at least appear to be, one hundred per cent confident at all times, unwavering in his dopey optimism.

"The show practically performs itself. All you gotta do tonight is go out there and give it to them," Thomas will say. "Need anything? Water, a beer, a smoke?"

You'll point to the half-drunk beer between your legs. "Drink-wise, I'm fine," you'll say, "but..."

"But what?"

"Know what I really need right now?"

"What?"

"A gun."

He'll put on a goofy smile, the neutral one he uses whenever he doesn't get a joke but is trying to hide it.

The gun won't really be a joke, though.

Something will click in Thomas's head. He'll draw up a chair, turn it toward you, sit. "I know it's a big night for you," he'll say, his voice more serious now.

You'll do him the courtesy of turning to look at him,

but it'll take so much effort you'll feel like you've just run a half-marathon.

"But I know you're gonna nail it," he'll say. "You always slay, bud. Everybody loves you right off the bat."

Everybody but yourself. Everybody but me. You'll curse yourself for thinking of me as soon as Thomas says the word "love," but you can't help it.

"It's weird, though," you'll say, "since *I* hate everybody."

"You don't gotta love them as long as you give them what they want."

"I dunno if I'm able to."

Thomas's smile will stay the same, but a panic he can't hide will show in his eyes. Halfway between fear and fury, he'll say, "Able to what?"

"Can we take Laurie's jokes out of the show?"

"Huh? But, like, do you even remember who wrote what?"

"It's my show, Thomas. Mine. All mine!"

"Well, no, Raph. It's not all yours. It's Daniel's too. He's footing the bill, so—"

"The show's constantly evolving. We cut stuff, we rewrite. It's all part of the process—"

"We can talk about this tomorrow, but now, tonight, keep doing what you've been doing for months. We're not gonna change a winning formula a half-hour before the premiere. Anyhow, this conversation is one to have with Daniel or even Sylvain, not with me."

Thomas will be right. Of course he'll be right. You and me didn't write the show joke by joke. It emerged from our two brains simultaneously at a lakeside cottage in one week, days when we connected like you've never connected with anyone ever.

You'll recognize that your request is absurd and childish,

but you can't help yourself. Ideally, you'd like to tear down what we've built and start over. Maybe even rebuild somewhere else. In another country. Far, far away.

"It's not a winning formula if it makes me wanna shoot myself in the head when I go onstage."

"And you're just telling me this now?"

He'll stand, run a hand over his hair, which is stiff with pomade. Open the mini fridge under the counter. Take out a can of Perrier, guzzle the whole thing. Turn to you. He'll open his mouth to speak, stop, let out a squeak. Breathe slowly. Then: "Raph, I'm *begging* you, don't sabotage this. Things were going so smooth. I thought we'd killed off that goddamn slacker persona of yours. I don't know what's come over you, but whatever it is, it's not good."

"It's been like this for five months, man."

"Five months? What, you mean *Laurie*?"

You'll shrug. Giving a clear answer would take too much energy. It'll be like gravity is suddenly a hundred times stronger. Or like you're on the ocean floor with the weight of all that water bearing down, slowing your movements, crushing your entire skeleton.

"You better get your shit together, bro," Thomas will say.

"I know."

"It's not normal."

"I know."

"Everyone gets dumped."

"I know."

"It's gotta stop."

"If you wanna suggest a solution, I'm all ears."

Thomas will turn in circles, like a dog chasing its tail. He'll stare at the floor, rub his face, then whip his empty Perrier can across the room. "For fuck sake!" he'll cry.

The stage manager, who's appeared in the doorway, will freeze in place. "Twenty minutes to showtime," she'll finally say.

You'll turn to her, give a big smile. "Twenty minutes. Thanks, Kelly."

Thomas will watch her leave, then close the door to the green room. He'll go into the fridge again, take out a Stella Artois, open it with the edge of his phone, throw the bottle cap on the floor. "So what do you want me to do?" he'll say. "Go onstage and announce that on the night of the Montreal premiere of his first one-man show, Raph Massi has flaked on us and everyone should just go home?"

"The issue's not even that." Your eyes will close by themselves. "Right now," you'll say, "I'm just trying to drum up the energy to lift myself out of this chair."

"Have you taken something?"

"No, I'm just on my second beer as usual."

"You need anything else? Are you going through withdrawal?"

"I've got coke if I want any. I've got everything I need."

"So what's the matter then? Jesus Christ, it can't be that you can't bring yourself to go onstage just because your girlfriend dumped you five fucking months ago."

"She's here tonight."

"Okay, so she's here. There are two thousand people in the house, Raph. You won't see her. I really doubt she's sitting in the front row. But if you want, I can go check the seating plan to make sure—"

"That won't work."

"Why the fuck not?" He'll be flushed, breathing hard, sweat beading on his forehead.

"It'll be worse if you ask her to leave since it'll mean she's won. She'll know she's still fucking with my head."

"Can we back up a bit?"

You'll shrug again.

"When did she tell you she was coming?"

"I saw on Instagram that Claire would be here."

"Claire. Who's Claire?"

"A friend of hers."

"And this Claire said she was coming with Laurie?"

"Laurie's in her story."

"Listen, I don't know how to say this, but, like, why the hell didn't you realize before tonight that Laurie would be here? Obviously she'd be here, you moron. She wrote the show with you."

"I was busy with other stuff, so I just, like, didn't catch on. It's only hitting me now."

"You realize what you're putting on the line?"

"Thomas, I'm just...sapped. I can barely move a muscle."

"I can go get that gun you want," Thomas will say. "Just shoot yourself in the foot, since that's what you're doing here."

You won't know what to say to that.

"It doesn't even seem to bother you," Thomas will add, "that you're throwing your career away."

"I know it's bad, man." You've never said anything with as little conviction in your life.

The door will open and Daniel will come in. Dapper. An extra button of his shirt undone to reveal a tuft of salt-and-pepper chest hair. Flushed cheeks and nose. Cheerful-looking, but winded and a bit tipsy. "How's our guy?" he'll say.

Seeing Daniel, Thomas will at first freeze, then straighten up and take a swig of his beer. "He's doing great," Thomas will say. "I was just gonna leave him alone to focus."

Daniel's eyes will jump between you and Thomas. He'll shake his head. "What's going on?" he'll say dryly.

"Nothing," Thomas will reply. "Everything's, um, under control."

Daniel's goofy cheerfulness will promptly vanish. His face will harden. "Nothing's going on and everything's under control. It sure looks like that," he'll say.

You'll turn to him, your jaw now weighing a ton. "I'm having second thoughts," you'll say.

"Second thoughts," Daniel will repeat.

You'll nod listlessly.

"You getting cold feet, Raphaël?"

Your nostrils will dilate like a bull's. You'll breathe out hard through your nose.

"Is there a reason for this?"

Thomas will rest his butt against the counter, stare at the opposite wall. "It's Laurie," he'll say.

"The scriptwriter?"

"Yeah, his ex-girlfriend."

"What's up with her?"

"Apparently she's in the audience tonight."

Daniel will throw you a look, baffled, full of scorn. "Look, sorry to bring up the money issue, pal," he'll say, "but you gotta understand your actions have consequences. Serious consequences. If you don't go out onstage tonight, you'll be royally screwed. By me and the entire industry."

"Okay."

"Royally screwed and left without a penny to your name. We're at Théâtre St-Denis, Raph. Your tour's supposed to recoup what it costs you to fill this place for free. And if you don't go onstage tonight, your tour will be pretty much scrapped, that's for fucking sure."

143

"Some people put their tours on hold because they're sick or burned out."

"You're not sick or burned out. You're just a goddamn little boy who craves attention. And I'm your producer, not your mom, even though I admit the roles can overlap. So you're gonna put on a smile, go out onstage, pretend to love life, and tell some jokes, because plenty of people out there have it way worse than you do, and your job's to help them feel a little less shitty for two hours."

"It's really, really not possible to just...postpone?"

"You should've choked *before* you stepped into the ring, kid. Fuck, if your mother died or you got hit by a car, I'd gladly send out a touching press release. But a breakup? Get over it! The number of guys, man, who'd sell their own mothers to be in your shoes."

"Well, they can have my shoes."

"You could fuck a different girl every night. And it's obviously not because you're so good-looking. I know a hundred guys sexier than you that don't have half as many women lusting after them. You could fuck a different girl every night, and you throw a hissy fit because your ex, some worthless nobody who's not even that hot, is in the house tonight? Grow up!"

You'll try sitting up straighter, but you've lost all your strength, so you cross your arms on the counter and lean your forehead against them. "I'm sorry, man," you'll mumble. "You bet on the wrong horse. I'm so sorry."

"Forget me for a sec. I'll be okay. You aren't my only client. I can pay my bills. I'll be fine. But consider this for a minute: when you became a comedian, you should've known you were also becoming a small business. And your decisions don't affect just you. Like I said, I'll be fine, I'll survive, I can cover my losses. But what about your manager here?"

Thomas will force a smile, a tense smile. "Yeah," he'll say. He'll keep rubbing a hand over his face while staring at the floor and shaking his head. He'll look like he's got early Parkinson's.

"He'll be the one stuck cleaning up this mess. Good luck finding another producer, my friend. You'll get nowhere fast. And the venues! The venues that book you rely on sold-out comedy shows to buy their goddamn boring contemporary-dance shows they program at a loss. They'll be up shit's creek. And what about your TV series in development? Keep this up and the production will be cancelled and fifty people will be out of their jobs. Including the young production assistant who makes fifteen bucks an hour, hopes for a career in showbiz, and thinks you're so nice and so human and so down-to-earth, even though you make five times his annual salary. All these people will get a kick in the teeth because you're just a frigging spoiled brat so desperate for attention that he can't stand it that some girl, for once in his life, isn't down on her knees begging to suck his dick."

Daniel's face will be beet red. The counter will be covered in his spittle. He'll stand immobile, staring at you, panting, looking ready to pounce.

There'll be a knock on the door. You'll straighten up, slide a hand over your clothes to smooth them out. Throw a glance at the mirror to see how you look. Your reflection will confirm that you're a professional bullshitter and that, even under the worst circumstances, you can look absolutely, completely, totally normal, ready to leap out onstage, tell jokes to two thousand people, and keep them enthralled.

"Yes?"

The door will slowly open, pushed by the stage manager, who stares at Thomas and Daniel with the eyes of a doe about to be eaten alive. "It's, um, ten minutes to showtime," she'll tell you.

"Ten minutes, thanks," you'll say as cheerfully as possible.

Thomas will take a deep breath, let it out slowly through his mouth, his eyes shut. Then he'll open his eyes, look straight into yours. "I know it's tough losing your girlfriend, Raph," he'll say. "But don't throw away everything you have left."

Thomas, you'll realize, is way more convincing when he talks business.

YOU'LL GO OUT ONSTAGE. OF COURSE YOU WILL. THOMAS will be right: working will be all you have left, so might as well throw yourself into it headfirst. It's incredible what the energy from a crowd can do. Once the stage manager gives you your five-minute call, you'll go wait in the wings and listen to Max wrap up his opening set. You'll hear two thousand people laughing and, what's more, being silent together. A fire will ignite in you. An electric current will shoot through your body. Your hearing will sharpen and your vision will tunnel, a reaction triggered by the reptilian brain, like you're being chased by a grizzly. A feeling of imminent death.

You never feel like dying just before you step onstage. We never feel as alive as when we feel death nipping at our heels. And even though it's not enough to mend your broken heart, your ability to get laughs, to shock and surprise, and to be loved by two thousand people simultaneously will be a consolation prize you can accept.

When the reviews come out the next day, they'll range from very good to glowing. They'll praise you for being comfortable onstage, affable, lighthearted, unpredictable, over-the-top.

But you'll hate the two reviews that mention the intelligence of the script.

"Everyone changes scriptwriters. It happens all the time," Thomas will say. "Your show's success isn't due to Laurie."

But you didn't have any real success before me, so you'll

have a tough time believing him.

Thomas will never bring up your backstage meltdown, but his behaviour will change somewhat. He'll become even more concerned about you, even more attentive to your needs. People are nicer when you make them realize they can get the heave-ho at any time.

IT'S AFTER MIDNIGHT WHEN THOMAS ARRIVES.
As he passes people, he shakes their hand, looks them in
the eye, all very professional. Thomas treats every party like
he's networking at happy hour. He waves to you, comes over
to us. Earlier I suggested we go join Claire on the dance floor,
and normally you'd never agree to dance, but since the idea
was mine, you didn't dare say no. Already, tonight, you're
letting me take the lead.

Thomas wedges himself into the sweaty crowd, lays a hand
on your shoulder, then wipes it on his pants, a bit grossed out
because your T-shirt's sopping wet. He yells over the music,
"Hey there, bud!"

"You got here late."

"I had dinner with friends of Sophie's."

"Oh, cool."

I kiss Thomas on the cheek. "Hi there, Thomas."

"Have we met before?" he asks.

"I work for Forand."

"Oh, yeah, of course."

He turns to Claire. "You work there too?"

"No, I'm a nurse on sabbatical," she says.

"Oh, so what are you doing here?"

"Is this party off limits to civilians?"

"No, no, that's not what I meant."

"Just joking," Claire says. She lifts her beer in the air,
dances in a circle.

Thomas laughs stupidly, not knowing how to react, then

asks you how your set went tonight.

"Pretty good, I think."

"Your stuff's really polished now. So time to write some new material."

"I'm working on it as we speak."

"Yeah, looks like it," Thomas says. He glances around, trying to hide his discomfort. He likes places that are ventilated and clean with assigned seating and clearly defined areas. A house party in a grungy apartment is less his scene. "Do you have any beer?" he asks you. "I came empty-handed."

"I must still have some left on the balcony."

Max Lap, who's just behind us on the makeshift dance floor, squeezes into our circle by butt-checking Thomas, who goes flying.

"Jesus Christ, Max!" Thomas yells.

"Okay, somebody's overdue for a beer," Max says.

The guys head off together to the kitchen. Claire disappears into the crowd. A bubble closes around us.

"Is he cool, your manager?" I ask.

"I guess," you say with a shrug. "Thom's a pretty nice guy. He's learning on the fly, but it's all good, I think. Of course he's not Forand."

"But do you really wanna be with Forand?"

"I dunno. Every comedian with Forand seems to be catching fire."

"That's true," I say but roll my eyes.

"What?" you say, your brow furrowed.

"Well, Forand *is* really devoted to his clients. But that's a good thing and a bad thing."

"How's it bad?"

I probably wouldn't talk about this normally, but I've been drinking and I trust you. We're feeling pretty good, you and me, intimate, standing close together in a tight crowd, so I say, "Well, if you ever do anything scummy, Forand will make sure it doesn't blow up in your face."

"How?"

I take a big swig from my bottle of wine but avoid looking at you. "If you only knew," I say, "the number of times I've had to send hush money to girls who were pissed at our clients."

"Really? Which clients?"

"I'm not paid enough to know which ones. It's better that way. I'm just given an address to send a money order to."

You glance toward the kitchen window. Outside, on the balcony, Sam's still chatting up the same girl as before.

"I guess if it's just the assistant taking care of it," I say, "it's like it never really happened."

YOU'LL WAIT IN VAIN FOR THE DAY WHEN YOU WAKE UP not thinking of me.

You've traded in the Gregorian calendar for a calendar starting the day of our breakup. On the seventeenth of each month, you'll remember it's been exactly one month, two months, three months, four months, five months since I left you. You'll show extraordinary restraint and not write, phone, or contact me even once during this time.

You'll keep me awhile as a Facebook friend, but seeing pictures of me looking happy on a trip, seeing pictures of me happy, seeing pictures of me period will eventually hurt too much. You'll decide it's better to unfriend me. Still, sometimes, without being my friend, you'll notice me liking or commenting on a post, and just seeing my name will have the power to ruin your day. It'll be a window into my world. Or a crack that appears in a dam and ends up bringing the whole structure crashing down. As you read my comment, you'll see the phone I typed it on, you'll see my fingers, my hands, my whole body, the sofa I sat on, my living room, my apartment, the dude who sleeps with me there, the places where I go with him, and this will be enough to spoil your entire day. The only solution you come up with will be to block me. To survive, you'll just need to pretend I never existed.

But a few weeks after your show opens, you'll have a moment of weakness. You'll contact me—by email since you've blocked me on all other platforms—and ask if I'll meet for a drink.

We'll arrange to meet at the bar downstairs from your place. You'll see me come in, and it'll annoy you that I look as pretty as ever.

"Sorry I'm late," I'll say as I sit down.

"No worries."

When you invited me out, you'd hoped to play it cool, be the guy who doesn't give two fucks, but you'll realize you aren't that guy at all. Seeing me a few feet away will be a kick in the face.

"How are things?" I'll ask.

"I feel like hanging myself and I'm on antidepressants."

The waitress will arrive just then to take our order. Because she overhears your comment and recognizes you, she'll clearly look uncomfortable. "What can I get you?" she'll ask.

"A Perrier for me," I'll say.

"A pint of blond," you'll say.

The waitress will scurry off behind the bar. She'll gossip with a co-worker and point in your direction. You still haven't realized that acting like a dick in public is a luxury you can no longer afford.

"A lot of people seem to recognize you now," I'll say.

"Yeah."

"You should be careful what you say in public."

"Okay, so everything's super-duper then, Laurie. Everything's fucking amazeballs."

I'll sigh. You'll figure that now I'm sorry I accepted your invitation. I'll be doing fine. I didn't suffer much after our breakup, as far as you can tell, so it never really crossed my mind to check on you, whether directly or indirectly. If I'd heard you'd gone crazy, I probably would've avoided all this awkwardness and turned down your invitation, but now you'll have me trapped and I'll be forced to listen to you, especially since you've played the mental health card and I'd look like a monster if I walked out after you just exposed yourself that way.

"I didn't say that so you'd pretend to be doing fine," I'll say, more caring now. "I just meant that, well, there's a time and place for everything."

"We'll only ever see each other in public, so I don't know where else I could've told you."

"That's why you wanted to see me?"

"No, but I felt like telling you anyway."

"For what it's worth, I don't think you should go through with it."

"What? Hang myself?"

"Yeah."

"Thanks. I'll keep that in mind."

Nothing will be easy. You'll fling every sentence at me like a dart. You'll realize that the couple on the Tinder date at the next table is getting a kick out of watching us. They'll eavesdrop, whisper about our conversation. Who can blame them, though? We're an excellent icebreaker, two tense exes having it out. Especially since the guy's Raph Massi, the up-and-coming comic everybody adores.

You'll turn to them. "Laugh all you want, guys," you'll say, "but in two or three years, you're gonna be in the same place we are now, and then you won't find it so funny. So maybe just zip it and stop staring."

I'll sigh, feel uneasy. I'll give the couple an apologetic look, and they'll roll their eyes and turn slightly away from us.

"I thought you wanted to see me to talk about work," I'll say.

"You saw the show."

"Yeah and you were excellent."

You can barely utter a thank you. Anything more and you'd start bawling.

"The staging was great too."

"Okay."

There'll be a lull in the conversation. I'll grow impatient and try to gently prod you to get to the point. "So what's up, Raph? Why'd you want to see me?"

Your nose will tingle on the inside like you're about to cry. "I'm just trying to understand," you'll say.

"I told you already."

"I still don't understand. What exactly...? Why'd you...? It's like I just can't wrap my head around it. The reason you did it. I don't get it, Laurie."

"I told you, Raph. I just...stopped loving you."

"But why?"

"Not everything needs a reason, y'know."

"But there *was* a reason, wasn't there?" you'll say.

"No."

"You just stopped."

"Yeah."

"Just...stopped."

"Yeah."

You'll lean forward, rub your hands together. You'll look psycho.

You've always been a bit psycho.

"I have another theory," you'll say.

The waitress will set the beer and Perrier down in front of us.

You'll knock back a third of your pint in one go. Then, you'll say, "You envy me, Laurie."

"You believe that? Really?"

"You left me because you envy me. You wish you were me.

You wanted to be a comedian, but it didn't work out, so you turned to comedy writing instead. Then you saw me onstage and got envious, so you left me."

"No, Raph."

"No?"

"I mean, well, I can't really prove it since there's no way to explain these things. But, like, all I can say is it wasn't envy. I just fell out of love. There's no plot against you or some major flaw that'd explain all this. There's just one thing, Raph, and I told you: I felt like I'd been propping you up for two years. And I finally couldn't take it anymore."

You can't argue with that, so you'll finish your beer in silence. I'll make up an excuse to leave.

You'll order a second beer and a third and cry into both. At the end of the evening, you won't have to pay your bill. As the waitress takes away your empty glass, she'll say, "Looks like you've had a hard night, so your drinks are on the house. Now go get some sleep. I bet it'll do you good."

Life's a series of missed opportunities. When you're poor and unknown, nobody gives you anything for free. When you reach the stage where you get things for nothing, all you want is a little peace and nobody will give you that.

YOU'LL BE SOLD OUT TILL THE FOLLOWING SUMMER. You'll soon pay back Daniel's production costs, and real money will start flowing in. You'll have enough to buy a new condo in Griffintown. Plus you'll take a trip to Thailand, though you can't be away more than two weeks since Thomas has booked you solid. You'll figure the trip will do you good, but you'll come to realize that taking a break is still dangerous because it leaves you time to think. And when you have time to think, you'll inevitably think about me. So just six months after you start touring your one-man show, you'll throw yourself into the writing of a second show.

Or you'll attempt to. Because without me, things won't be the same. You'll try hard, though. You'll rent a cottage on the same lake as my aunt's place in Eastman. You'll pop Ritalin every day for a week. You'll sit down in front of your laptop at seven every morning, ready to write non-stop, but nothing will come. The magic will be gone.

At the end of your two-week stay, you'll have one new bit, only one and a crappy one to boot, on boomers and their iPads. A few days later, you'll test it out at Le Bordel (yes, the club will now welcome you with open arms, practically roll out the red carpet).

Your new bit will fall flat.

In the first few seconds of your act, it'll dawn on you that the bit has probably been done a hundred times, and no doubt a hundred times better.

"What I find fascinating is that the boomers I know are all super loyal fans of the iPad. They do everything on it. Talk to their grandkids, take photos of the Eiffel Tower, show their photos of the Eiffel Tower in a loop to their guests, monitor their money on BMO's banking app while lecturing you for not working hard enough. But what I find kinda touching is that not a single boomer knows how to properly work an iPad. It's like watching a three-year-old use an Etch A Sketch."

You'll imitate a little kid concentrating hard as he madly twists the knobs of an Etch A Sketch. You'll get a few smiles, maybe even a giggle, but nothing more.

You'll realize your bit's as lowbrow as Larry the Cable Guy joking about Walmart. You've become what you've always hated.

You'll lower your mic, scan the crowd. "I'm so sorry, guys," you'll say. "A gag that lands that bad makes me wanna off myself."

That'll get a laugh. Before you press on with the rest of your set, you'll follow that trail to see where it leads. You'll figure the evening's already a flop, so it can't get any worse.

"I said 'off myself,' but maybe it could be suicide *lite*. Basically, all I want is for you to witness my death and feel real bad for not laughing at my joke."

The fish will swim toward the hook. More laughs. Forced laughs, awkward laughs, but laughs all the same.

"You'll all gather around my coffin in two weeks saying, 'Oh, if only we'd laughed at his joke, maybe he'd still be here.'"

The fish will take the bait.

"That's what happens when you watch *The Butterfly Effect* one time too many."

You'll regret that comment, figuring the movie reference is

too obscure, that few people will make the link. No one will react at first, so you'll feel you should've quit while ahead, that you went from recovering the puck on a penalty kill to scoring on your own net. But a half second later, the time it takes for everyone to make the mental leap to baby-faced Ashton Kutcher, the crowd will roar, satisfied not only with your joke but also with the niche reference from their adolescence, which they'd forgotten.

You'll barrel on ahead.

"Anyway, I'm just kidding myself. You won't gather around my coffin. I'm not famous enough. But if, say, John Mulaney died, you'd probably be happy provided you got an invite to his funeral."

The crowd will laugh again, for several seconds, and you'll even get some applause.

"You'd take a selfie. Like, 'Tag your friend who would've gone with you to see John Mulaney's next show in Montreal.'"

You've reeled in your fish.

You'll get back on track afterward like nothing happened, and you'll catch a second wind. The audience will now be all warmed up and willing to follow you wherever.

Later you'll be leaning against the bar when some dude will come up and buy you a beer. "Killer set," he'll say. "When you went off on that suicide tangent at the start, I pissed my pants, man."

The guy pissed himself laughing.

You'll keep going off on that tangent. You can't not. You won't necessarily feel like it. Maybe deep down you just dream of telling poop jokes. It might do you good to offer up comedy that lets people think about nothing in particular, exist outside their world. Pure escapism. But everyone loves when you're inappropriate and dark.

You'd be nothing without an audience. So better give the people what they want.

You'll build a bit that starts with a deliberately lame joke (the gag about boomers and their iPads, or some other drivel depending on your mood), you'll do your riff on suicide to guilt-trip your audience for not laughing at your stale joke, then you'll say you know it's horrible to talk about suicide, that it makes everybody uncomfortable, but it's still a useful skill to develop in life, for example, when you hold an intervention. You'll tell the story of Renaud, your suicidal friend who you and your buddies had to keep a watch on and how it'd go when you'd spend evenings with him.

"Y'know, all of a sudden, you become super self-conscious. Like you really wanna have a conversation with the guy, but you feel that any little slip-up might trigger him. Say you tie your shoelaces in front of him. Will he start thinking about hanging himself?"

That'll prompt little cries of mock disgust, the kind telling you that you've gone too far, and at the same time, they like it because they might've once had a moment of weakness, lacked empathy, and briefly had the same thought. It's cathartic. People pay you to go too far for them. To be offensive by proxy.

"The thing is, when Renaud started doing better, we all stayed paranoid. One time, he slipped away from a party, after saying he'd *had enough* and was *dead* tired. So I got nervous and called the cops to go check on him, and my poor buddy got his front door battered down by, like, a SWAT team. I wish I could tell you I made that up."

You made that up. You've got no friend named Renaud.

This bit will be an instant hit. Whenever you go onstage, you'll feel like you're popping a big balloon with an X-acto knife. Like you're opening valves shut tight for twenty years and the pressure's released all at once. Like you're naming something no one else has dared to name.

But people don't have these thoughts when they see stand-up. They might say your show's funny, but don't expect them to write a freaking thesis on your artistic approach. That's the great thing about comedy: people come to laugh, and if they laugh, they're happy. It's not rocket science. We just have to get people laughing. It's simple. Not easy. But simple.

When Thomas sees your new set for the first time, he'll take you aside in front of the club after the gig. He'll give you a cigarette, then cup a hand around it while lighting it.

"Everything okay, bud?" he'll say.

"Yeah, fine. Why?"

"Nothing, nothing. Just wondering."

"I'm fine, Thomas. I tell jokes, people laugh. So things are good."

"You do more than just tell jokes, though—"

"I know, I know," you'll say. "I have an approach, I tell stories, blah blah blah. But all I mean is that right now people love me. How could things be bad?"

It's the easiest way you'll find to reassure him.

"Are you worried because if I hang myself, you'll have trouble making the payments on your cottage?"

"Raph."

"It was a joke."

"Save it for your set, alright?"

"Okay, boss."

As with all the material you create alone, you'll take a moment to wonder if I could've written anything as good. And for the first time ever, you'll honestly believe the answer's no. You'll honestly believe you're smarter than me. For the first time ever, you'll believe you're better than me, and that'll make you feel damn good.

YOU'LL GET FOUR NOMINATIONS FOR THE OLIVIER COMEDY
awards that year: Comedy Show of the Year, Olivier of the
Year, Radio Feature of the Year, and Newcomer of the Year.
You've always claimed not to give a fuck about the Oliviers,
mostly because deep down you didn't want to get your hopes
up, but once you're nominated, you'll suddenly be all keen
on winning.

Thomas will be waiting for you on the front plaza outside
Radio-Canada, sweating in the big Kanuk puffer you got as
swag and pawned off on him. He'll give you a hug, then rub
a hand over your freshly shaved cheeks. "Someone's finally
learned to use a razor," he'll say.

"My barber strong-armed me. Said I couldn't go to a gala
looking scruffy."

"You look handsome, dude. C'mon." He'll drag you to the
front entrance, saying, "Let me know if you want me to stick
close by or give you some space."

"I dunno what I want, Thomas."

"Well, just keep me posted."

Inside, the place will be crowded. You'll try to find a direction to look in that lets you shut down a bit, but almost everywhere you glance, there'll be someone you need to smile at or
nod hello to.

Thomas will lead you to the backdrop printed with the
Olivier logo. A lot of cameras will be pointed at you, and you
won't know which one to look into. You'll smile stupidly.
You'll pick Thomas up like a bride and pretend to plant a kiss

on him. Everyone will lap it up and snap your picture.

Thomas will spot Sam in the crowd, wave him over to be photographed with you, then he'll move aside, and Sam will drape an arm around your shoulders.

It'll be a great photo. It won't surface much the day after the gala, but later it will. Later it'll blow up.

Sam will change poses. "You realize we're both Olivier nominees?" he'll say. "Can you fucking believe it?"

You'll smile and say, "Thanks for not competing with me in the radio category at least."

You'll be up against Sam for three of your four nominations. This will be the first time you feel you've beaten him at something. The first time you feel you've gotten the last laugh. Still, nominations mean zip if you go home empty-handed.

You guys will head to your seats. You'll be sitting together— you, Sam, Thomas, and Forand.

Forand will lean over to you. "Getting nominated is already a big deal, Raph," he'll say graciously. "Be proud of yourself."

When Forand turns to face the stage, Thomas will glance your way. "Forand's shitting his pants," he'll whisper.

"But it's true what he said," you'll say.

"Yeah, yeah, it's true. But are you gonna tell me you wouldn't be happy to upstage Sam for once?"

"I dunno," you'll say. Then you'll add, "Hey, it's like you wanna stick it to Forand as much as see me win."

Mariana Mazza, the comedian sitting beside Thomas, will give you the stink eye. Thomas will smirk at you, then slide a hand into the inside pocket of his blazer, take out a flask, hand it over. Gin.

It'll burn your throat but relax you just enough so you can act like you couldn't care less who wins.

The host for the ceremony will be Pierre Hébert, but you'll

barely register a thing the guy says. You'll zone out. When the people sitting around you laugh, you'll copy them, though with a quarter-second delay. You'll wake from your stupor only when you hear, "And the nominees for Newcomer of the Year are..."

The screen at the back of the stage will play clips from the shows of all the nominees: you, Sam, the little mean girl who does stand-up for woke university students, the guy who always looks like he's on mushrooms, and the guy who claims he's gifted and talks about his "curse" for an entire ninety-minute show, while forgetting that comedy's supposed to contain actual jokes.

"The winner is...Raphaël Massicotte!"

You'll feel your blood pressure drop. You'll stand, go up onstage, spend the first ten seconds giggling like a maniac, then say, "I wanna take this opportunity to tell my high-school guidance counsellor he should really find another job because, according to him, I would've made a really good social worker. First of all, no, I would've probably caused irreparable damage. Second of all, does anyone ever take a career test and get told they should be a stand-up comedian?"

Genuine laughter throughout the auditorium, plus a big round of applause.

"Also, Sam..." You'll point in his direction, though you can't see him given the stage lights. "I just wanna say I'm sharing this with you. You're such a pain in the butt that the jury probably decided to give me the prize as a reward for putting up with you since our first day at the comedy school."

You'll get off the stage, disappear into the wings, go back and sit down next to Thomas, placing your Olivier trophy between your feet.

"It's all good now, bud," Thomas will say. "We got

everything we needed. It's crazy!"

"Congrats, dude!" Sam will add, giving you a fist bump. "You fucking deserve it."

The flask of gin Thomas passed you will be empty. You won't have time to get more booze because the winner of the Comedy Show of the Year will be announced and you'll hear them call your name again.

You'll feel a bit more dazed onstage this time. The alcohol has dulled your brain. "Wow!" you'll say. "Was my show really that good, guys?"

A whoop will ring out from the back of the auditorium, followed by applause.

"Anyway, I obviously want to give a shout-out to the entire team behind the show—the production people, the director, also my manager, who's gonna be insufferable at the party tonight. And big thanks to all the jury members I sucked off."

Big laughs from the audience.

You'll think of me for a moment. You haven't thought of me for a few days. That's how it'll be after a while—you'll think of me less and less frequently. At first, I'll be on your mind every minute, then every hour. But by this point, you can sometimes go days, even a week, without thinking of me—a miracle.

But now, you'll think of me. You'll lose yourself in the vastness of the auditorium, wondering if I might've been invited inadvertently. Might I be out there in the audience, a short distance away, without you knowing?

"A big thanks to everybody. Really."

Obviously you won't do me the honour of saying my name.

You'll stand there, a bit wobbly on your feet, wondering what to add, but you'll feel paralyzed simply because you just thought about me. Your big mouth will go numb, and you'll find nothing smart, or funny, or surprising, or even stupid and inappropriate to say.

You'll just lift your trophy in the air and head off the stage. The music will start up one beat too late, a slight delay, nothing uncomfortable, or awkward or anything, just a hiccup in a ceremony that has otherwise run smoothly.

After you leave the wings, you'll stop at the bar rather than go directly back to the auditorium. The bartender will be staring at his phone, but when you stand your Olivier on the counter, he'll glance up and say, "Hey, congratulations."

You'll force a polite smile. "Can I get a glass of blond?" you'll say. While he pours your beer, you'll turn toward the empty lobby to avoid his stare and fend off any small talk. You'll hear him set down your plastic glass behind you.

"My treat," he'll say. "I really dig what you do."

You'll nod at him. Anything more would require too much energy.

You'll chug your beer.

Thomas will text you: "Where the fuck are you?"

You'll grab your trophy, head back into the auditorium just as it's announced you've won the Olivier of the Year.

You won't know where to put the trophy you're already holding, so you'll carry it back onstage. You'll be standing in front of the entire audience a third time, now with two Oliviers in your hands, not to mention the one you left at your seat.

"If somebody had told me five years ago that I'd be here tonight..."

If somebody had told you five years earlier that you'd be where you are that night, you would've thought you'd at least be happy. And what strikes you—as you struggle to finish

167

your sentence and stare out at the people in the auditorium, who are equally impressed and resentful given your big haul of trophies—will be that you feel nothing.

You'll lean toward the mic and let out a burp. The audience will erupt in laughter. You'll take a big bow, like you're Kent fucking Nagano, then leave the stage.

People will laugh. People always laugh, whatever you do.

IT'LL BE THE SECOND-LAST TIME YOU SEE ME.
Thomas will drag you to the little Olivier studio so you can be photographed with your trophies, and he'll stop you just in time from miming that you're shoving one of them up your ass. Afterward, he'll watch nervously as you're interviewed by reporters, finally loosening up a bit when you're done.

Daniel will bring you a beer and rub your shoulder, looking very pleased. "It was well worth it to throw that little tantrum on the night of your premiere," he'll say with a smirk.

You'll consider smacking him in the face with a trophy, but instead, you'll just knock back the beer he gave you and hand him the glass. "Thanks a lot, Daniel," you'll say.

"I told you your show would work."

André, Max Lap, and Sam will drag you back to the photo area to take group shots. They'll lift you horizontally, then drop you because you go too limp to be held up.

Sam will help you get back up. "Will you ever forgive me, man?" you'll whisper to him.

He'll look you in the face and smile. "It's party time," he'll say. "Let's get trashed."

On the way to the party, André will give you your first few bumps, and you'll immediately realize it was time you started in on the coke because the room was spinning around you. The coke will make you a bit more stable and keep you from puking. It'll also help you speak in more than just monosyllables.

The party will be packed. Usually, you can weave skilfully

past people you don't want to talk to. But that night, everybody will want to interact with you, even when you walk off in another direction after spotting them, even when you turn away from them, even when you ignore them. People will need to tell you they love you and think you're awesome. They'll take selfies with you and your Oliviers. They'll lean in too close, their warm breath smelling of mint and beer. They'll stink of sweat. They'll kiss your cheeks, their skin clammy, or rough, or greasy. It'll be extremely unpleasant.

You'll survive, though. You'll be congratulated and told you're the man of the hour so often and do so many hits in the bathroom with André, Sam, and Max Lap that you end up believing that, hey, maybe this night *is* yours.

Then you'll spot me.

I'll be sitting discreetly in a corner, not taking up much space, smart enough to know not to set you off. But, still, I'll be there. Because the place isn't a private club, after all, and everyone connected in some way to the industry will be there that night. It won't be so unusual. It'll be natural for me to be there.

Ordinarily, you'd feel sad to see me. Your shoulders would slump and your eyes would soften. You'd want to melt to the floor and disappear from the room. But that night, no. Your muscles will stiffen, lava will course through your veins.

Before you have time to think, your legs will be moving in my direction. Before you have time to make a decision, you'll be inches from my face, screaming like a hyena: "What the fuck are *you* doing here?"

I'll be gentle with you. I'll know not to provoke you. I'll still know you well enough to know that when you're in a rage, I should speak slowly, flatly, lower my eyes, do everything to calm the beast.

"Hey, Raph," I'll say.

"You're on my fucking turf here!"

"I..."

"My turf!"

Within seconds, your eyes will well up.

"My turf! Mine! You have no business coming here to stalk me. Were *you* nominated tonight?"

"Well, technically with your show—"

"No, you weren't nominated. Because you're a fucking nobody. Without me, you're nothing. The only reason you managed to work for even two minutes in comedy is because I talked you up. And what've you done since we split? Fuck all! FUCK ALL! Because you're worthless. You're just a fucking leech!"

As you wave your arms around, you'll almost hit a waiter with an Olivier trophy.

"Raph, you need to calm down," I'll say as respectfully as I can.

"Calm down?"

"If you can."

"CALM THE FUCK DOWN?"

I'll be the only one who can see how hideous you look. The muscles in your neck will be so taut that the shape of your windpipe is visible. The veins in your temples will stand out like on an old lady's hands. You'll be covered in sweat like you've stepped out of a sauna.

"Calm down? FUCK! Easy for you to say. Have *you* ever raised your voice? You've fucking got the upper hand, with everyone saying, 'Laurie's so nice, Laurie's so perfect, Laurie's always so chill.' You have everyone wrapped around your finger, and I'm so goddamn sick of it. Everyone thinks you're so fucking smart and perfect. But I know the truth.

The truth? You're a fraud. I *know* you. You aren't a good person, it's a fucking front. You get off on watching people, judging them, cutting them down. You're envious as hell, since the only talent you've got is scrutinizing and criticizing everyone. It's easy to be all aloof and superior when you never put yourself on the line. But Laurie, I lay myself bare. I do it even if I might fall on my face. And guess what—it's paid off. It's fucking paid off. Because look at this!" You'll wave an Olivier in my face. "I've got this and you've got nothing. You're fucking nothing."

"Raph," I'll say. "I think you need to get some help."

"Great, just great! When you run out of arguments, just say I'm sick in the head and you get the upper hand."

Someone will lay a hand on your arm—tenderly, not threatening at all.

"Raph, let's go for a smoke, okay?"

It'll be Sam. He's never been so gentle with you. You'll stare at him, then realize you're panting, so you try to slow down your breathing. You'll look back at me. Take a step, just one step, a small step in my direction. "People like me now, Laurie," you'll say in a much quieter voice. "People like me."

Sam will lead you to the exit, smiling apologetically at everybody around you, though you barely notice.

After you push the door open, you'll feel like you've taken your first real breath in two hours. The cold December air will make you realize you're practically drenched in sweat. Even though you feel like retreating into your shell, bursting into tears, screaming your lungs out, you'll have to make do with just holding your breath and clenching your teeth really hard. After all, you'll be with Sam, and it's not okay to cry in front of other people.

172

You can't look him in the face. You'll stare at the city lights in the distance, the cars driving by in the street.

After a while, Sam will break the silence. "That went well."

"Thanks."

"I was joking."

"Fuck you."

He'll offer you a smoke, let the flame flicker in front of your face. You'll inhale, the nicotine as jolting as a cold shower.

"Wanna call an Uber?" Sam will ask.

"Why?"

"It's after two a.m."

"So what?"

"I think it'd be a good time to go home."

"What the hell are you talking about? A good time to go home? What's your fucking problem?"

"Raph—"

"She's not gonna win, that bitch."

"I just said that so—"

"This is my turf. Mine! She's not gonna drive me away from my own turf. Not on the night when I've won big."

Sam will try to hold you back, but you'll push him away. Your vision will be blurry, but you'll just follow the bass back to the party. You'll bump into everybody in your path. When people don't move away fast enough, you'll elbow them, just because you can. You'll knock at least two beers to the floor and splash red wine down the white blouse of an influencer, who you'll call a ditz.

You'll hide out at the bar, order a double gin and tonic.

"How are you paying?" the bartender will ask.

"It's an open bar."

"No, it isn't."

"It's an open bar for fuck sake!"

"No, sir, it's not."

"I fucking won. I won big time. I deserve a drink!"

You'll take the drink without paying, give the bartender the finger, then head to the dance floor. I'll be there. You'll come up to me, lift your drink in the air, sway your hips. Like we're just two people, any two people, partying down. I'll turn my back to you, move away. You'll grab my arm, turn me toward you, then let go.

I won't move, I'll just stare. Maybe I'll figure it's the safest thing to do. Maybe I'll be scared to death.

You'll get all up in my face. "You're such a shitty human being," you'll say, just loud enough for me to hear you over the music.

You'll stop seeing the night's events play out. You'll just retain a series of isolated images: my back, lost somewhere in the crowd; bottles lined up perfectly behind the bar; Thomas's questioning look and his hands gripping the back of your neck; one of your Oliviers standing on the toilet-paper dispenser; your shoes covered in vomit.

Images will start to link together again only once you find yourself sitting in a taxi with Thomas and his girlfriend. "Where we going?" you'll ask.

"Home," Thomas will say.

"There's no after-party?"

"Nope."

You'll lean your forehead against the window. Replay the evening in your head.

You'll have a moment of clarity, then start crying. You'll whimper like a baby, your head still against the window. "Laurie's a fucking cunt," you'll whine.

Thomas's girlfriend, sitting up front, will throw you a worried look.

Through your tears, you'll mumble, "Don't you guys agree?"

Thomas will glance uneasily at his girlfriend.

"Admit it that what she writes is fucking crap," you'll say. "Thomas, you know it. You saw almost everything she wrote."

He'll take a deep breath, then say, "It's true she didn't revolutionize comedy."

Just hearing those words will make you feel warm inside.

"HOW ARE YOU DOING?" THOMAS WILL ASK WARILY. HE'LL basically know the answer, but he'll be angling to assess the extent of the damage.

You'll be kneeling in front of the toilet bowl when you get his call. Dry-heaving and throwing up bile for the fourth time since you woke up. There'll be nothing left in your stomach, but you'll still be retching.

"I won three Oliviers," you'll reply. "How do you think I'm doing?"

There'll be silence on the line. Then a breath or a resigned sigh, which you won't hear. You'll be busy controlling your breathing so you can survive the pounding you feel in your temples with each beat of your heart.

"It was a big night for you."

"Uh-huh."

You'll get up. Put in your AirPods so you can free up your hands and wash your face.

"What are you doing now?"

"Washing my face."

"Oh, okay."

"I don't have anything scheduled this morning, do I?"

"No, no."

"I was scared you called to say I'd forgotten some commitment."

"No, no."

Another silence.

"Can you tell me what happened last night?" Thomas

will ask.

"You were there. You should know."

You'll see yourself for the first time since you got up. It won't be pretty. The first thing that jumps out will be your black eye.

"Did I get into a fight?"

You'll notice a smudge of dried blood on your right hand.

"No, not that I saw anyway."

"Too bad."

"But it wouldn't be surprising."

"I have a black eye."

"Maybe when you got out of the taxi last night. You fell. I dunno."

"I hurt my hand too."

As you examine yourself closer, you'll see your face is covered in tiny red and purple dots forming a Zorro mask around your eyes. You've vomited so much you've burst blood vessels. And your skin underneath will be grey and translucent. A dribble of vomit has dried on your cheek.

"I probably can't do TV for a couple days. Not without thick makeup at least."

"You don't have any TV in the next few days, Raph. It's okay." He'll take a deep breath, then add, "You can't always do that, y'know."

"But I don't always. Last night was a special occasion. I won three Oliviers."

"Raph."

"What the fuck? It was the Olivier gala, dude. There's always some troublemaker causing a scene. This year it was me."

"Yeah."

"Did I do anything really bad, though? Anything criminal

that could get me in hot water?"

"Other than simple possession of cocaine, no."

"But everyone there was guilty of that."

"Yeah."

"So stop freaking out."

"Raph, you can't act like that in public."

"I wasn't in public last night."

"Yes, you were."

"Well, we comics aren't exactly upright citizens. Everyone knows we're a group of narcissists fighting for attention."

"Not that kind of attention."

"Have you read the news? All it says is I won three Oliviers. I won three Oliviers and that's it, man."

You'll want to say more, but you'll be forced to stop talking to slow down your breathing. Your headache will now be worse, your temples throbbing so much you have to close your eyes.

You'll lean against the sink. "I won three Oliviers, Thom," you'll say. "I won three fucking Oliviers." You'll hunch over, then add, "I'm nice enough to keep my mouth shut and pretend everything's fine so you can pay for your cottage. So if one night I let loose, can you cut me some slack?"

"You weren't just celebrating. It was more than that."

Your head will pound harder, your stomach will heave, your throat will open wide. You'll squat in front of the toilet, grip the rim of the bowl. Your whole body will clench painfully, all your muscles contracting. You'll retch violently, but only a long string of bile will come up.

"Raph? Are you okay?"

You'll sit on the floor. "Overall, no, Thom, I'm not okay."

There's a crinkling sound on the line—the rustling of Thomas's blazer, probably freshly pressed, as he shifts in the leather chair in his office. You'll feel under threat, so to hit back, you'll drag Thomas onto what's shaky ground for him—talking about feelings. And you'll hope for a second that he veers from his usual conversations with you, that he tells you that he gets why you acted so horrible at the party, not that it makes your behaviour any smarter, but he gets it. Maybe he'll say he knows he can't do much, but at least he understands, he knows you acted that way because you're basically crazy and it doesn't embarrass him to admit it. Maybe he'll say you're crazy, but it's not so bad, you guys can deal with it, there's a way, because crazy people like you, you're everywhere.

But he won't say any of that. On the line, there'll just be the faint sound of him wetting his lips nervously as he wonders what to say. "But you shouldn't feel bad," he'll finally come out with. "You said so yourself. You should be proud of your big win last night."

"I don't want you managing me anymore, Thomas."

"What?"

Another rustling of his blazer, but more frantic this time.

You'll get up, wipe your face, then stumble to the kitchen to pour yourself a glass of water before Thomas makes another sound.

"Raph, I'm gonna let you get some rest. You had a big night."

"Fine. You'll let me know how to go about breaking our contract, if there's stuff I gotta sign."

No rustling now, but a tense silence, a sound of breathing.

"Raph, you're tired. We'll talk about this after you rest up."

"No, man. I know what I want. I don't want a nutjob as a manager anymore."

"This is a decision that requires some thought and discussion. You really should mull it over a bit."

"There's no talking to you. I've thought about it plenty. I don't want to work with you anymore."

"You won't last two days without me organizing every part of your life."

"I'll find somebody else. I mean, I just won three Oliviers, so I'm sure to get somebody decent, right?"

Silence.

"Can you at least tell me why?"

"Things don't always happen for a reason, Thom."

Sounds from the room where Thomas is sitting. A distant siren.

"Okay. I have two of your three Oliviers if you're looking for them. We can write each other about the practical matters."

Around two in the afternoon, your phone will start ringing non-stop. You'll figure, oh no, you must've committed some crime at the party and reporters now want you to comment, defend yourself, confirm the facts. Instead, though, you'll have three messages from talent agencies calling to offer you their services.

Forand will be one of them. "Listen, Raph," he'll say, "it was a real pleasure seeing you last night. It's always a pleasure, always. And I'm so happy for you, I sure am. Like I said at the gala, you deserve it. I predicted you'd win big, it was so obvious, just crystal clear to me."

There'll be a half-second pause.

"Listen, I heard about Thomas. It's too bad because I know you had a good relationship. But if ever you want to join our agency, we could take you on. I've always loved what you do. The two of us could make a good team. Anyway, congrats again for your Oliviers. Get back to me about a meeting."

You'll text him: "You should've signed me when I got out of school."

OVER THE NEXT FEW DAYS, YOU'LL TRY TO ACT LIKE everything's fine. Nothing will be fine. Everyone will be chasing after you on account of your Olivier wins. You'll have to answer your own phone and speak to human beings. Your secretarial skills, however, are almost nil. You'll have to set your own alarm clock and estimate your own travel times. You aren't good at either. You'll have to sign contracts, negotiate fees. The last time you did any math was back in high school in a remedial class.

You'll miss an interview on the morning show *Salut Bonjour* and turn up two hours late for a shoot. You'll notice that something's changed when no one blows up at you or even calls you out for being late. People will want you, so they'll just have to deal.

You'll arrive at ten to eight for your show in Joliette because you mistakenly thought you were performing in Brossard that night. You'll turn up at a fitting where none of the clothes are your size given that the measurements you sent the wardrobe supervisor were just estimates. The woman will be furious. You'll blame your former manager, say he was completely useless and that's why you fired him. When she shows you that the email she got was from you, you'll just say that the bungling manager you fired was in fact yourself. That'll make her laugh, and all will be forgiven.

At age twenty-six, you haven't managed your own schedule or finances in five years. You haven't made your own appointments with the barber or dentist, haven't deposited a single cheque. You haven't had to resolve any scheduling conflicts or phone back production coordinators to confirm that you'll show up somewhere. Thomas was your buffer against any unnecessary hassles from people whose jobs wouldn't even exist if we all agreed that everything in life could be settled with a two-line email rather than with five four-hour meetings and three conference calls with Toronto. This shield against all practical matters might be your biggest luxury purchase in life.

After two weeks of hell during which you spend half your day on phone calls and emails rather than doing what you're usually paid to do, you'll crack and decide you really do need somebody to replace Thomas. But getting a new Thomas would be too much bother, so you'll just go see the old one.

"Let's get one thing straight," you'll say to him. "You don't tell me what to do, okay?"

You'll be at his apartment, standing between his bed and worktable. He'll stare at you, parked in his chair, frozen in place. He'll be wearing sweatpants and an old T-shirt. You haven't seen him without a blazer on in at least three years.

"I'm the boss, okay? If we decide to team up again, Thomas, I'm the boss."

"Okay."

"You don't tell me what to do. Your job is to take me as I am and deal with it."

"Okay, Raph."

"Not to put me in some fucking box."

"Okay."

"You tried to do that and things went south."

"So why do you wanna start up with me again?"

"Because I know you've got a cottage to pay for and you'll shut your trap."

"I'm not doing so badly, Raph."

"Yeah, right. How many managers sign their deals beside their dirty underwear?"

Thomas's eyes will drift to the pile of dirty clothes next to you on the floor.

"We were in a hurry and didn't have time to do laundry, so—"

"If you're not interested in my offer, you can just say no, Thom."

"Why does your offer sound like a threat?"

"I'm not in your head, man. If you feel threatened, that's your business. Talk to your shrink about it."

"No, it's not that. It's just, like, I thought you and me had a friendlier relationship. I mean, we're buddies and that's why it worked."

"Well, maybe that's the problem, Thom. We mixed business and friendship. I don't wanna be your buddy, I don't need it. What I want is somebody who can book my appointments, negotiate my fees, tell off anyone who screws up, and, especially, mind his own fucking business. Are you the man for the job?"

"Um...yeah."

"The question you should ask yourself is do you need the money?"

Thomas will scan his apartment, let out a sigh.

"It's not like you've got a promising roster of clients," you'll add.

"I've got Martine."

"Martine has trouble filling three nights at Zoofest, and she does radio pieces on breastfeeding on shows no one listens to."

"She's about to break out."

"Dude, she's been doing the same thing for ten years. If people were interested in her, we'd know by now. She's not a stand-up, she's a mommy blogger."

"I've got Jean-François."

"Thomas, the guy's been banned everywhere."

"Not everywhere."

"He compared Pierre Karl Péladeau to a pedophile live on Radio-Canada."

"Yeah, but it was a joke."

"The lawyers didn't find it so funny. Anyway, I'm not sure you'll make much money off a comic who describes himself as anti-capitalist."

Thomas will get up and pace around the little empty space in his bedroom. "It's just, like, I don't want any trouble, Raph," he'll plead.

"Maybe you should've become a civil servant then."

"Can you just promise me one thing?" He'll stop in front of you, almost breathless. "Can you try to quit drinking? Just try it and see? It might help you feel better too."

SOBRIETY WILL BE PURE HELL FOR YOU.

You'll delete that phone number Sam gave you and dump your bottles of booze down the sink.

There's no preparing for this. Nobody can. We've all grown up with alcohol, it's part of our daily lives, so for it to become a banned substance overnight isn't normal.

The first days won't be pretty. Every morning, you'll get out of bed not having slept a wink that night. You'll have to wash your sheets every day because you sweat like a pig in them. You'll get the shakes too, but they won't last that long.

The hardest part? No one's ever shown you how to do stand-up sober. You've only done it five times tops, and never by choice, only because you knocked over your beer or you arrived at a gig too late to throw back a few before showtime.

No one performs sober by choice. That's what you'll tell yourself as you pace around the green room the first night you have to do your act without a drink. Time will pass slower than usual, and your blood pressure will keep climbing in the last half-hour before you go on. You'll try watching Max Lap's set from the wings, but it won't distract or calm you. You can't be in the moment. You'll just stress about your perfor-mance, alternating between rehearsing your act in your head and telling yourself you need a beer pronto, ASAP, right that minute, or else you'll die.

You'll manage to do your set, of course you will. But you'll move like a rusty robot onstage. Your whole body will feel out of joint. You'll have trouble responding to what's going on in front of you. You'll have a filter.

A filter! You, the guy whose stock-in-trade is going too far, saying the wrong thing, being inappropriate, over-the-top, too much. A goddamn filter! Sometimes, when you lay into a member of the audience, some bitchy comment will be on the tip of your tongue, but you'll stop a second and think, Should I say that? Should I really say that? and rather than spit it out, you'll swallow the insult.

It's not like your show will be ruined. It'll still be good, that's not the point. It's just that any pleasure you could possibly feel onstage will be gone.

Also gone will be any other possible topic of discussion for you. You'll still need maybe two new bits to round out your next show. You've kept the material on suicide, which Daniel likes since he can now sell you as having a voice that's more mature, more reflective, darker. There's an audience for that.

Anyway, after your Olivier wins, you could suggest doing a drag show and he'd be all in.

Sobriety will now be all you can talk about. How your days are long, your nights even longer. But no one wants to hear how boring your life is. There's maybe a way to make people laugh at a dark, desperate life, yes. But a boring life? It's just not sexy.

One night at Le Terminal will be especially embarrassing.

"Hello there, everybody. Very happy to be here. But just, um..." You'll make a little pouty face. "Before I start, I dunno if you'd mind removing any alcohol from your table. Just so it's not in my line of vision. Because I quit drinking a couple months back and find it tough even to *see* alcohol."

You've heard more laughs at a funeral than after that joke.

"And don't go chugging your drinks, because that'd be

even worse. Maybe just, I dunno, pour them on the floor. I think the staff will understand since, y'know, I have a medical condition."

Not one peep from the audience.

"The thing no one tells you about sobriety is that it's fucking boring, right? Look, I've got my schedule from the past week here..."

You'll take a sheet of paper out of your pocket. Already this gag will seem too scripted, too staged. Audiences don't like that. They like spontaneity. They want to see you make things up on the spot. You'll be lying to them.

"Monday night: drink herbal tea, organize shoes, be in bed by eight. Tuesday night: drink kombucha, watch *Property Brothers*, be in bed by eight. Wednesday...okay, time to crank up the fun: drink green tea, hire a hooker, be in bed by nine."

Crickets again. Normally, with two beers in you, you'd just scrap that bit, laugh about it with the crowd, roast yourself, poke fun at your audience to cancel out the jokes that bombed. And that'd result in a really good performance. But that night, you'll just stand there watching the train speed toward you, hoping it mows you down quick.

"As for interacting with other people, only now that I'm sober have I noticed how totally boring everyone is. Why is that? You alkies and druggies don't know how lucky you are. One beer's good, the conversation flows. Ten beers and it's like you're chatting with a friend from high school. A quarter gram of coke and it's like you've just found yourself the best business partner ever."

A polite laugh, the first of your set. But you probably got it just because a good chunk of your audience knows you and will *want* to be enjoying your act, even though they aren't. They'll pity you, feel bad for you.

"I've thought a lot about this and I've come to a conclusion: the problem's not drugs and alcohol, it's *quitting* drugs and alcohol. So just stay reasonably drunk or high every day of your life and you won't have a problem."

This might draw a chuckle, but nothing more.

You'll pause to look out at the crowd, scan from left to right. A good ten seconds will go by, enough time for people to fidget in their seats. "Guys, let's be honest," you'll say. "That bit sucks ass."

Now everybody will crack up.

"Listen, I'm gonna go home and clean my apartment. I'll come back if I find the crumbs of my talent that I lost down the side of my couch."

The bartender will throw you a look of concern when you pass her on your way to the green room. The crowd will applaud politely. One woman will grasp your arm and say, "It's okay, Raph."

You'll hurry away. Sam will be lounging in the green room when you come in. "You're already done?" he'll ask.

"I feel like slamming my head against the wall, Sam."

"What went wrong?"

"Everything, man."

"We'll go out after, okay? You'll forget about it."

You can't say you don't see a bit of sadistic satisfaction in Sam's face. He'll head off to do his set while the host tries to recoup and boost the energy in the room after your fuck-up. You won't want to go watch Sam. From the green room, you'll hear people laughing uproariously almost as soon as he starts performing, and that'll already be enough to make you die inside.

Sam will hang out at the bar after the show because some female fan will be desperate to talk to him. You'll hole up in a corner drinking your Perrier and staring at the floor to avoid the looks of pity and contempt.

Finally, Sam will come over with his little admirer. "Let's bounce, dude," he'll say. "Soleil's coming with us, okay?"

FORAND WILL JOIN YOU GUYS AT THE BAR. SINCE SAM makes no effort to include you in his conversation with his young fan, you'll be forced to talk to his manager.

"All's good with Thomas now?" Forand will ask.

"Yeah, yeah."

"He's a cool guy, Thomas."

"Yeah."

"Not very aggressive, but he's cool. A bit misguided sometimes too, not necessarily the best negotiator, but he's cool. He's really cool."

"Yeah."

Forand will stick out at the bar, not that he'll notice. The dude's in his mid-forties at least, while the second-oldest client there will be, like, twenty-eight. "You hear Sam's news?" he'll say.

"What news?"

"He's hosting a gala this summer."

"Oh, yeah?"

"Yep! They didn't approach you?"

"Nope."

"That's a surprise. With the exposure you got after your three Oliviers, you'd expect they would have. Thomas didn't think you might like to host?"

"Well, the guy's not God. There's only like, what, five galas?"

"A good manager has to be at the right place at the right time, y'know."

You'll smile as if you agree because that's clearly what he wants and you don't have the energy to argue. He won't be satisfied unless you admit you can't sleep at night since turning down his offer to manage you, that you regret saying no, that now you dream of working with him.

"But I'm sure we can at least wrangle you an appearance at Sam's gala. The two pals from the comedy school together again, that'd be fantastic. Anyway, you've got new material, right?"

"Yeah, I do."

"You performed something new tonight, didn't you? How'd it go?"

"Poor Raph! He didn't even finish his set." Soleil will slip into your conversation like a punch in the face. You'll suddenly realize you were maybe lucky to be chatting just with Forand.

"He was *so* adorable onstage. Poor guy!"

You'll roll your eyes, annoyed, but she'll keep going. "But, hey, you bounced back, Raph," she'll say. "And the crowd was on your side."

You'll stare at her awhile. There'll be something very adolescent about her. "Hey there, uh, Soleil is it?" you'll say.

"Yeah, it's Soleil."

"Are you even old enough to get into Le Terminal?"

She'll hold a finger up to her mouth, kidding around that you should keep quiet.

"Maybe you just don't have the maturity yet to understand the jokes of us grown-ups," you'll say.

She'll burst out laughing, then snort like a pig. "You see," she'll say. "Now *that's* funny!"

Sam will arrive with four shots. Seeing you, he'll shake his head. "Oh, shit, I totally forgot," he'll say.

"It's not like I'm always talking about being on the wagon," you'll say.

"Well, that just means an extra one for us," Soleil will say.

Forand will turn to Sam. "How was your set?" he'll say.

"Pretty chill."

"He was AWESOME!" Soleil will yell.

The girl will get more and more tanked, start slurring her words, and have trouble focusing her eyes on anything. She'll nuzzle Sam's neck, kiss him.

"I'm gonna hit the road," you'll say. "Two hours sober in a bar is my limit."

"Can you give us a lift?" Forand will ask. "I've been drinking, so I shouldn't drive."

"Um, I guess so, but those two, you sure they wanna go home?"

Sam and Soleil will be sucking face openly at the bar. Forand will signal to them that it's time to leave. They'll stop making out but stay wrapped in each other's arms.

Though you feel contempt for the girl, it'll still be touching to see how Soleil looks at Sam. She can't stop staring at him. Her pupils will practically shimmer with admiration.

She'll look at Sam the way we're looking at each other right now. That's what'll come to mind when you see Soleil like that. A little lump of sadness will form in your throat. But it'll be okay since there's no better place than a crowded bar to hide how you feel.

It'll be ages since you've looked at a girl, or a girl has looked at you, that way. People have much less sex once they stop drinking. We forget that two beers can give just the right amount of courage for hooking up.

Sam and Soleil have had way more than two beers. They'll follow you and Forand out into the street.

Weirdly, Forand will become more controlling, more businesslike. "Raph will drop everyone off," he'll say.

"Oh, it's okay, we'll catch a cab," Sam will say, exchanging a knowing look with Soleil.

"No, Raph will drop you off."

You'll glance at Forand, who'll remain stoic. You'll walk toward your car. Behind you, Forand will keep an eye on Soleil and Sam. He'll help them into the back seat, then get into the passenger seat. Once you're behind the wheel, you'll say, "Where we going?"

"I live on the South Shore," Soleil will say with a hint of shame.

She'll live with her parents in Saint-Bruno. Of course she will.

"But we're not going to the South Shore," Sam will say with a hint of pride.

Soleil will giggle. "Oh, yeah, I…"

"Soleil's coming over for a nightcap."

Forand will nod yes, as if to himself, his lips pursed. A moment later, he'll say, "But Raph could take you home no problem."

"What?" Soleil will say.

"Raph could take you back to your place if you want. If ever you change your mind on the way to Sam's, it's no big deal. Raph's sober."

You won't even look at Forand. Something insistent in his tone will be almost scary.

"Okay then," you'll say. In the rear-view mirror, you'll see that Sam has slipped a hand into Soleil's bra. "Should we head to Sam's?"

"I live closer," Forand will say. "Drop me off first."

You'll stare at the road in silence, your car gliding past the snowbanks on either side of the street. Man, would you ever kill for a drink.

You'll arrive at Forand's place. After he opens the car door, he'll say, "Soleil, take down Raph's number."

"What?"

"Take his number."

"Why?"

"If you change your mind, Raph will come pick you up and drive you home. It's no trouble for him since he hasn't been drinking."

"But why would I change my mind?" Soleil will ask.

Forand will throw you a stern look so you don't ask questions. You'll give your number to Soleil, who'll type it clumsily into her phone.

You'll have no idea what's going on.

"Thanks, Raph," Forand will say as he steps out of the car. "Good night, Sam. Good night, Soleil."

As you head to Sam's, you'll realize it would've made way more sense to drive there before going to Forand's. Forand planned it so he'd be dropped off first.

When you get to Sam's, Soleil and Sam will practically tumble out of the car, then stagger to the front door. They'll wave to you and yell, "Thanks!"

You'll see them kissing in front of the door before they go in.

When you wake up the next day, you'll have six missed calls from the same number and a voice message. When you call back, it'll go to voice mail. In a bubbly tone, Soleil will say, "Hey, it's Soleil! Don't leave a message, text me instead."

THE CROWD HAS THINNED OUT A BIT, AND FEWER PEOPLE are dancing. Most of the guests are huddled in the kitchen, smoking joints or cigarettes under the range hood. You and me have plunked down on the couch to carry on talking. I'm showing you pictures of my trip to Iceland (the pictures I didn't post online since you've obviously already seen the ones on social media).

We're sitting side by side. Our shoulders are touching, and our knees a little bit too. You've had a hard-on for an hour.

A loud crash comes from the crowded kitchen. Everyone turns in that direction. A bottle of beer has broken and spilled across the floor. Someone you don't know, a youngish girl standing in the middle of the kitchen, lurches away from the mess she's made. "I'm so sorry, guys!" she wails. "I didn't mean to!"

Hands on her shoulders, Sam leads her away from the spill and into the living room while André, still hopped up on coke, is happy to have a job to do and orders everyone out of the kitchen so he can pick up the shards of glass and mop up.

"Yo, everything's chill," Sam says to the girl. "It's just a beer."

She sniffs, nods, looks unsure. "Okay, thanks," she says. "You're so sweet."

Elena Miller comes up behind Sam, nudges him aside. "It's okay, Sam," she says. "I'll take care of her."

"No, it's chill."

"No, Sam, I'll handle this," Elena says sharply.

Sam smiles but looks taken aback. "Why you being so aggressive?" he says.

"I'm not being aggressive, Sam. I just mean everything's fine. I've got this. I'll put her in a cab."

"But we were going home together."

"Listen, you can hook up another time. She's in no condition right now—"

The girl glances at Elena, then at Sam, then back at Elena. "But everything's chill now," she says, looking pretty out of it.

"We were just about to leave," Sam says.

Elena crosses her arms, exasperated. "Leave her the hell alone, Sam," she says. "I dunno what else to say to you."

"Really, you're being totally hysterical," he says.

You turn to me, feeling uneasy. "Wanna get going?" you say.

"RAPH, SHOWTIME IN ABOUT AN HOUR," THE STAGE MAN-
ager will say after knocking on the door frame to get your
attention. You and Thomas will turn to her. "And Sam wants
to see you in his dressing room," she'll add.

"Right now?" you'll say. "Because we have a bit of a
situation."

The stage manager will shrug and head off.

Thomas, his AirPods in his ears, will look up at the ceiling
and go back to his conversation on the phone. "I just sent
you his measurements," he'll say. "If you have something,
anything that looks a bit dressy, can you bring it to us in—"
He'll turn to you and mutter, "How long did she just say?"

"An hour."

He'll go to the craft basket, take an apple, bite into it, then
carry on with his conversation while pacing around your
dressing room. "The gala starts in an hour," he'll say. "Raph
got screwed and has to perform first, so he goes onstage in
like an hour and fifteen minutes, an hour and twenty. If you
can take pictures of what you're bringing and send them, I
can get approval right away from wardrobe and the director.
Uh-huh. Uh-huh. I know. The easiest way will be to come by
taxi, so you won't have to park. Keep your receipt of course. I
owe you big time, Jen."

Thomas will hang up, let out a groan. "My back aches from
bending over backwards for these idiots," he'll say. "You have
no idea."

Another knock at the door. A bored-looking hipster will

be leaning against the door frame. "Hey, the production coordinator told me to come see you."

Thomas will turn to her. "Who are you?"

"Héloïse, the wardrobe supervisor."

"Oh, so you're the person. We have a problem. Raphaël, stand up. Put on your jacket."

You'll comply without a word. You've met the wardrobe girl, Héloïse, only once before when she suggested a houndstooth suit to you in keeping with the chic look of Sam's gala.

"What's the problem with the jacket?" she'll ask.

"It *vibrates*," Thomas will say cuttingly.

"Vibrates?"

"Onscreen, it vibrates. Look, we won't get into optical theory tonight, honey, but all you gotta know is that houndstooth might look sharp, but the check pattern vibrates so much onscreen that it looks like Raph's sending coded messages with his suit. Obviously it's not visible here, but during rehearsal, I looked at the monitor and his suit was vibrating like a damn tuning fork."

"Okay."

"I thought it was maybe just the monitor, so I asked the director, and he'd noticed it too. He said he can't put something like that on air. It hurts the eyes."

"Because it vibrates too much."

"That's right. I even spoke to the producer. He watched it and said that, in any case, they have to edit out material to fit the TV time slot for the gala. So anything ugly onscreen is sure to get cut."

"Okay, listen, I can see what we—"

"Look, the show starts in an hour. I'm not gonna make you work for nothing. Raph's stylist is on her way here with some other options—"

"But there's still an aesthetic to respect—"

"Jen will have a few outfits you can choose from—"

"It's not just me. The director has to give approval too. This suit was okayed two weeks ago—"

Thomas will lose his cool, raise his voice a notch. "Héloïse—it's Héloïse, right?"

"Yeah."

"With all due respect for your work, people haven't come here tonight to see the comedians' outfits. They've come to hear their jokes. So let me do my job and arrange it so my client doesn't end up on the cutting-room floor. Okay?"

Héloïse will roll her eyes, push her glasses up the bridge of her nose. "Alright," she'll say. "But you still need approval."

"I'll have the photos in a couple minutes. You can give your damn stamp of approval, I assure you. And by the way, none of this would've happened if you'd done your job right in the first place."

She'll sigh like an exasperated teenager, then stomp off down the corridor of dressing rooms. Watching her go, Thomas will shake his head and say, "Fuck, this is like some high-school production." He'll turn to you, rub your shoulders. "But everything's under control, bud."

"You think we'd have this kind of problem if *I* was hosting?"

Thomas will shake his head again. "But do you *really* wanna host a gala?" he'll ask.

"Totally."

"No, right now, you gotta focus on your second show. You can't be dicking around. And no bitching. After all, you got that article in *La Presse* with Sam. You've gotten almost as much coverage as the host. No one else got that."

True, the newspaper article published the day before was pretty good. The reporter traced your career paths since you and Sam got out of the comedy school. He portrayed you guys as the bad boys of a new generation of Quebec comics.

"Your show's your priority for now, Raph."

"Because it's not ready."

"Exactly."

"Because it's still missing something."

"I didn't say that."

"Daniel's not happy."

"Raph, it's a process. You know that—"

"It's just that the process is frigging slower and messier than with the first show."

"You've got some good material, though."

"Yeah, the stuff I wrote before I quit drinking."

Thomas will come sit down beside you.

"Raph, we've talked about this. It's for the best."

"How many sober stand-ups do you know?"

"After a while, it'll become second nature."

"After a while? How long exactly? It's been six months."

"You'll see, you'll get used to it."

"What do you know, Thomas? Have you ever tried to stop drinking, even for two minutes?"

"You wanna go back to how things were before?"

You'll turn to face the big mirror in your dressing room. It's true the houndstooth suit will look sharp. It'll almost make you look in shape, and your gut won't protrude from your shirt. You'll take the leather loafers that Héloïse found for you and set them down on the counter, then tilt your head back and sigh. A pig being led to slaughter, that's how you'll feel.

"Thom!" a voice will call out.

In the mirror, you'll see Jen dash into the room, arms overflowing with garment bags.

"Jen, you've saved our asses," Thomas will say. "You have no idea."

Jen will eye your jacket, then pat your shoulder. "Jeez, of course that thing wouldn't fly on TV," she'll say. "It's costume design 101."

Just then, Héloïse will walk by in the corridor. She'll hurry past your dressing room, and Thomas will close the door.

"So I found a couple things. The nicest is this black wool suit," Jen will say, unzipping a garment bag. She'll take out a jacket—very simple, a bit shiny. "The pants are only a thirty-two," she'll add. "But I have other options."

"He has to be comfortable in it," Thomas will say.

"They couldn't just let us dress normal?" you'll say.

"Baby, if we let you guys dress yourselves, you'd go onstage in plaid shorts," Jen will say with a chuckle. "You're not to be trusted."

She'll hand you the pants. "Want us to step out?"

"No, it's okay." You'll slip out of the houndstooth suit and put on the black wool.

Thomas will seem satisfied as he checks you out in the mirror. "Can you breathe okay? Are you comfortable?" he'll ask you.

"Yeah."

"Great. I'll update your measurements. You're a thirty-two now, not a thirty-four. It's crazy the weight you lose when you cut out alcohol."

The stage manager will knock again, then open the door partway. "Raph, did you go see Sam?" she'll ask.

"Oh, shit, no. Where's his dressing room?"

"I can take you there."

She'll walk at almost a jogging pace, weaving through the maze of corridors, iPad in hand, giving the once-over to everything she sees. To a technician, she'll call out, "Jonathan, don't forget we have a harness hookup at six forty-five."

"Noted."

She'll turn to you, say, "That's not your original suit."

"Long story."

She'll frown but won't question you further. The two of you will walk by a screen showing a shot of the stage, work lights on, technicians hooking a spotlight onto the grid. You'll feel your heart speed up. She'll finally lead you to Sam's dressing room, knock, then enter.

One of Sam's scriptwriters will be going over the cue cards with him. "The gag just after your story about the horny little dog, I think we can skip it since it's never landed," the scriptwriter will say. "And the cards for your hosting duties are here if you want to review them. I entered the corrections you asked for. If you have other changes, I can put them in the teleprompter."

Sam's dressing room will be twice the size of yours. There'll be a huge leather armchair and a hot-meal service, not just energy bars and sandwiches with no crusts. Behind Sam and the scriptwriter, a dresser will be on her knees, touching up the back of Sam's shirt.

The director will be leaning against the counter and going over notes in a notebook. Beside him, the producer will be nodding his head.

"No, that's too stripped down. It'll look cheap and lack texture. I want you to lower the tulle curtain—"

"Are we sure it'll be okay, given how the lighting is focused? We don't have time to link—"

The stage manager will cut in: "Sorry, but I need wardrobe approval for Raph Massi."

The producer and director will glance over at you with

dead-fish eyes. They'll both say, "Looks good," then look back down at the notebook.

"Raph!" Sam will look up from his cue cards and wave hello. He'll be rooted to the spot on account of the dresser behind him.

"You wanted to talk to me?" you'll say.

"Yes, is everything good on your end, man?"

"Oh, me, I don't have much to do, right? My face is on the poster, I'm on for eight minutes, then I'll bounce."

Sam will force a smile. You'll sense that he's stressed. "You'll do a super job," he'll say. "No doubt in my mind."

"You, you're good?"

"I still have a couple minutes left to freak out."

"If you do your opening like the other night at Le Bordel, you've got nothing to worry about, dude."

That show was, in your opinion, just okay. Tame, good-natured, a crowd-pleaser. Sam joked about the implausible plots of the films we watched as kids, like *Home Alone* and *Air Bud* with the golden retriever who plays basketball. Not groundbreaking bits. But a show like that does the trick when people have paid ninety bucks a ticket, want their money's worth, and therefore try hard to have a good time. And even you have to admit that Sam has really improved his delivery. He'll be more relaxed, yell less, speak slower. He'll be calmer.

"Thanks," he'll say to you. "The team has worked pretty hard, so I think it'll be a good gala. I'm so glad you agreed to come on the show."

Why all this small talk at a time when he'll clearly have other things to do? You'll have a bad feeling about this.

"I wanted to mention something to you..."

"Uh-huh."

"But I was so busy with the show I didn't have time."

"What's up?"

"I wanted to give you a heads-up."

"About what?"

"You might run into Laurie tonight. At the party afterward."

A jump into an icy lake. A cold that stops your breath.

"Oh."

"I invited her to the nine-thirty show."

"Why?"

Silence. Sam will look down at the floor.

"I wouldn't normally talk to you about this."

"About what?"

"I mean, it's not a hundred per cent sure."

"What?"

"I mean, not yet."

"What isn't?"

"Laurie's gonna work on my next show."

"As a scriptwriter?"

"Yeah. I figured it'd be better you hear it from me, rather than just, y'know, seeing it or hearing it from somebody else."

A quiver in Sam's voice will betray his real intention—not to protect you, but to make sure you aren't furious with him. You'll exchange a look with the dresser, who's still on her knees behind Sam.

"We can talk more about it," Sam will add, "when the time's right."

"No need," you'll say, teeth clenched. "Is that it?"

"Yeah, I just wanted to be sure I was the one to tell you. I know it's not the best setting, but..."

"It's okay."

"But after the show, we'll talk, Raph. We'll talk if you want to."

"Of course, Sam. We're friends. We'll talk."

"It's just that Laurie's so good, dude. You know it, you worked with her. She's one of the best. We started bouncing ideas off each other, and we just thought, Wow, why didn't we ever do this before?"

"Uh-huh."

"Anyway, it's been, like, a real long time since—"

"Yeah, it'd be stupid of me..."

"Yeah."

It'd be stupid of you to be mad at Sam for this. But never underestimate your stupidity. Never. Because the only way you've found to feel any better is to erase me from your life.

Sam will know it. He'll know that just hearing about anything related to me, even indirectly related, means you'll beat yourself up for days.

Sam will know. You can't see how he could've done this innocently.

You'll leave his dressing room with a tight smile, no longer aware of your surroundings. You'll shuffle like a zombie down the theatre's corridors. You'll knock into a production assistant and won't even think to apologize.

Jen will be collecting her garment bags and getting ready to leave when you arrive back in your dressing room. You'll make a beeline for the fridge, grab a Boréale IPA.

It'll go down cold and smooth, tasting like fruit and bread. It'll leave behind a bitterness, although not as strong as the bitter taste left in your mouth since you fled Sam's dressing room.

Thomas will give you a distraught look. You'll chug the beer while looking him in the face, then let out a loud burp. "You say one word, one fucking word," you'll warn him, "and I'll ditch you for Forand."

IT'LL TAKE ONLY THREE BEERS TO PUT YOU IN THE MOOD
to go onstage. You'll drink them alone in your dressing room
after Thomas leaves to go sit in the auditorium.

When you're in the wings waiting your turn and watching
Sam onstage, your pulse won't race and your breathing will
stay under control. You'll picture yourself going out onstage
to interrupt Sam's opening. He'd be confused, wonder why
you'd come on early. You'd punch him in the fucking nose.
He'd double over, bleeding in front of two thousand people.
You'd grab his head, knee him in the face. Hard. He'd spit his
teeth into the audience, his mouth a bloody mess.

Damn, that'd make you feel good.

"He's one of my best buds. We've been tight since the
comedy school. Real tight. Still, I'm afraid to get *too close* to
him since I suspect the dude has lice. Maybe fleas too. Nope,
not the cleanest guy around, but boy does he ever make me
laugh. Let's give it up for Raph Massi!"

You'll go out onstage bursting with big-dick energy. You'll
amble over to the centre of the stage, your gait smooth and
solid. You'll take the floor, your skin drinking in all the light.
You'll pause to size up the crowd, make each person think
you're looking them directly in the eye—them and only them.

"I'm back, bitches!" you'll cry.

You won't know why you said that, nor will the audience,
but everybody will burst out laughing at the same time. You'll
have them eating out of your hand throughout your whole
set. Home run.

Afterward, you'll hole up in your dressing room till your next performance. Your set will kill even more the second time, if that's possible. This time, to boost your confidence, you'll imagine yourself spitting in my face rather than punching Sam out.

You'll leave Place des Arts right after, instead of waiting till the end of the show. You'll figure it's a better option than running into me.

But you'll want to keep your buzz going and to party on. You'll sit down at a patio for tourists in the Quartier Latin and have another pint.

Your post-show beer is always the one that tastes the best. It's your reward. You've worked for it. You deserve it.

A girl will ask if she can take a selfie with you on the patio. You'll say yes. She'll put her face next to yours, hold her phone at arm's length. You'll plant a kiss on her cheek, which makes her laugh.

You'll start walking home. It'll be a mild night with a full moon. You'll feel great. You'll feel awesome.

But once your beer buzz wears off, you'll want to wipe out a couple images that have slowly formed in your mind—me and Sam behind our laptops in my aunt's cottage, me and Sam naked in bed.

Sam never mentioned anything of the sort, but you'll wonder if he was maybe speaking in code, or playing down parts of his story, to protect you.

You'll want to keep partying. Get totally shit-faced.

You often told me that Sam wasn't that respectful or nice to girls. You'll wonder if you should've said the opposite. Maybe the best way to keep me far from Sam would've been to say he's a nice guy.

You'll wonder if, after our split, Sam deliberately kept you away from me so he could then swoop in.

You'll wonder if I cheated on you with him.

You'll realize it's been three years since we broke up, that your rage is a completely immature, irrational, and stupid reaction to have. By this point, we haven't seen each other in a year. You won't know who I am anymore, and I won't know who you are either. Sam being with me instead of some other girl shouldn't make a difference. Yet it'll make a big difference. You'll remember you still love me.

You'll hate yourself. You'll hate yourself so much.

You won't recall the corner store's exact address. You'll just know it's on the south side of Mount Royal Avenue, somewhere between Le Terminal and the West Shefford. You were totally wasted the last time you went there, so your memory won't be crystal clear. Also, it was a few years earlier. Memories can fade with time—not all, but some.

You won't know if there are business hours, specific times you should show up, a specific employee you should approach. You won't give a fuck, though, because you've run out of options.

The walk there will be miserable since the sky has clouded over and rain starts coming down hard. Puddles in the street will almost overflow onto the sidewalks. Thunder will rumble at regular intervals, often right overhead. Every time you walk by a corner store, you'll glance inside and think, Nope, not this one. When you spot the right store, three blocks from the West Shefford, you'll know immediately. You'll know because you remember that the last time you went there, you felt like throwing yourself into traffic.

The front door will chime when you walk in. You'll stand stock-still in the entranceway, your clothes soaked through and dripping onto the floor.

The short cashier will be there. Maybe even dressed the same. Like he's spent three years suspended in time just waiting for you.

"I've bought matches here before," you'll say.

IT'LL BE AFTER TWO A.M. WHEN YOU SEE THE POLICE LIGHTS flashing in your rear-view mirror.

Before then, you'll spend an hour drinking at home and doing bumps on the kitchen counter. You'll eventually get bored and clean up your apartment with a beer in hand. You'll also sit in front of your MacBook to type out some ideas for a new comedy bit. You'll feel like your brain's working right for the first time in ages. There's a reason why people do coke. A good reason.

Around one a.m., you'll get tired of putzing around and decide to go out. Max Lap and André have texted you that they're with Sam at Just For Laughs.

You won't dare ask if I'm there too. But, regardless, you can't stay home. During your sobriety, the idea that people are partying without you will always gnaw at you, make you feel like a reject. You'll still feel the magnetic pull of a party. You'll usually manage to ignore it, but that night, after ten beers and a quarter gram of coke, you can't ignore it anymore.

"Don't know how much longer we'll stay," Max Lap will text.

"Be there in twenty minutes tops," you'll write back.

You'll tell yourself it's a bad idea, you might run into me and have another meltdown, the Oliviers version 2.0, or you'll see Sam and lose your shit or take a swing at him and then look like the biggest asshole ever. But, despite the risks, you'll still leave your apartment, go down to your car, get behind the wheel. Drive toward downtown.

To avoid attracting attention, you'll tell yourself to drive slow and not make any sudden manoeuvres.

It'll be after two a.m. when you see those police lights flashing in your rear-view mirror.

You'll count to three, hoping the lights aren't flashing for you, that the cops are just randomly driving in your direction, that they'll speed up and pass, but the police car will start tailgating you.

You'll be on Mount Royal Avenue. You won't get why you're on that street given that you were heading downtown.

You'll drive another block, just to make sure there's no misunderstanding. Just in case. You'll hear the siren blaring behind you.

You'll tell yourself nothing bad can happen.

You'll pull over very carefully. Smoothly. To show you're in full possession of your faculties. A guy who can parallel park perfectly wouldn't be asked to take a Breathalyzer.

The cop will amble up to your car, knock on the window. You'll lower it and give her your choirboy smile.

"Where are you off to tonight?" she'll ask.

"To work," you'll say.

"To work?"

"Yes, a work-related event."

"What kind of work do you do so late?"

"I'm a stand-up comedian."

She'll frown. Click on a flashlight, point it at you. Seeing your face, she'll waver a bit. She'll glance back at her partner in the police car behind you.

"Can I see your registration?" she'll say.

You'll open your glove compartment. For a good fifteen seconds, you'll rifle through old McDonald's wrappers and gas-station receipts till you find the document. You'll hand it over.

The cop will check it, a troubled look on her face. "Wait here, please," she'll say.

You'll go over your options. I'd like to say you won't consider getting out of your car and running like hell into the night, but that'd be a lie.

The cop will slowly walk back, lean over, and say, "Please step out of your vehicle, sir."

You'll stare at your steering wheel. A feeling of imminent death.

"Mr. Massicotte?"

You'll give a slow nod, place your hand on the door handle, push the door open. You'll stumble getting out, and the cop will grab your arm to steady you.

"Can you give me your keys?" she'll say.

"Oh, shit. They're in the car."

A group of teenagers will be watching you too closely, so you'll instinctively pull up the hood of your hoodie. The cop will lean over, pull your key out of the ignition. She'll raise the window and lock the doors using the key fob buttons.

"Come with me, please."

You'll go with her. She'll open the back door of her vehicle and ask you to get in. You'll buckle up, then promptly pass out.

"Is this your place?"

You'll wake up when the police car stops outside your apartment.

"This isn't where I was going."

"No, but it's your address, right?"

You'll nod, confused.

"You should go inside, Mr. Massicotte."

"You think?"

"Yes," she'll say. "Try not to do this too often. It could be bad for your career." She'll give you back your key and registration.

Her partner, in the passenger seat, will turn to you before you step out. "I really love what you do," he'll say. "Have a good night."

YOU'LL TELL YOURSELF NOTHING BAD CAN HAPPEN.
"Raph, are you at home?" Thomas will say on the phone.
He'll be speaking softly, which is worrying.
"Yeah."
"Can you come by the office?"
"In the flesh?"
Thomas will know you spend your weeks travelling around. He's cut your meetings in person to a minimum because your schedule's already packed. If he's asking you to drop by the office, something serious must be up.
"Yeah, if possible. I see on your schedule that you have a brainstorming session for your series at two. That'll give us time to have lunch."
"What's up?"
"We'll talk when you get here, okay?"
"Okay."
"And please switch off your phone."
"What?"
"If you can. Turn it off, okay?"
You'll hear in his voice that he's trying to reassure you. Trying but failing.
Just before you switch off your phone, you'll get a call from Sam. You'll stare at his name awhile on the screen of your iPhone and wonder what to do. You'll have an urge to answer, mostly because Thomas told you not to.
The decision will be made for you: you hesitate so long that Sam's name disappears from your screen.

A cold shiver will run through you, lingering even after you shut your phone off.

You'll turn hypervigilant. You'll be paranoid someone's following you. You'll be scared that a car will barrel into you with no warning, that a sniper hiding behind the curtains of a hotel window is waiting for you to step into view so he can gun you down.

You'll tell yourself nothing bad can happen.

When you get to Thomas's office, your T-shirt will be drenched with sweat. His assistant will greet you with a smile tinged with sadness. "Hi, Raph," she'll say with a sorry look, then lead you to the conference room.

Thomas will be seated in an armchair with two salads from Mandy's in front of him. He'll get up to shake your hand. He'll force a smile, but you'll see right away that he's got the look of a cow scheduled to be butchered that night. He'll take a deep breath.

"You didn't ask me here to share good news, I guess," you'll say.

"No."

"On a scale of one to the end of the fucking world, where does this fall?"

On the sofa beside him is an iPad, which he'll hand to you.

"It'll be easier if you just read this."

It'll be an email:

Below is a partial list of names compiled by individuals connected in some way to the Quebec comedy scene. On the basis of first-hand accounts, we are denouncing the men named herein for abhorrent behaviour involving one or more of the following acts:

—Sexual assault

—Grooming

—Soliciting nude photos
—Sending unsolicited nude photos
—Sexual harassment
—Physical harassment
—Exposing their genitals
—Persistent unwanted online contact
To protect the courageous victims who have come forward, we have not linked these men to a specific act. If you have any ties to the men, we ask you, for the greater good, to draw up a concrete plan to show that you in no way tolerate the acts listed above.

Your solidarity is essential so that drastic measures can be taken. Realize, however, that regardless of your response to our request, we will move forward with the next steps in our efforts to ensure zero tolerance for sexual misconduct in any form.

Note, too, that other names will be added at a later date.

Listed at the end of the email will be about twenty names. Names of men. Men you know. Including Samuel Bouvier.

"That's it?" you'll say.

Thomas will stiffen. "Raph, this is no joke."

"Okay, so you have reason to believe I should be on this list?"

He'll look uneasy, glance up at the ceiling, then out the window. "Well," he'll say, "since Sam's on it..."

"Since Sam's on it, I'm guilty by association?"

He'll force a nervous little laugh, then: "No, no, that's not it."

"Well then, why'd you use that grim tone of voice when you called me here? Like a doctor set to tell me I had ass cancer."

"We don't know what these people might do, Raph."

"These people write emails. That's all we know so far."

"Sam was just dumped by Forand."

You'll bark a laugh. "Don't mess with me, Thom."

"I'm serious. Sam was just dropped. I spoke to him. And TVA has cancelled his series."

"What? Two episodes have already aired."

"I know."

"But no one's even confirmed all this yet."

"Reporters are apparently working on the story right now."

You'll look absently out at the building across the way. Lost in thought, you'll finally mutter, "Jesus Christ."

"Yeah."

You'll look back at Thomas. "But am I okay?" you'll ask.

"I don't know, Raph. Are you?"

"I mean...I dunno." You'll suddenly feel out of breath.

Thomas, gentler now, will say, "Has any girl at any time ever..."

"How should I know? Yes, no, maybe—I mean I can barely even remember the sex I had three days ago."

Thomas will rub his eyes.

"Has any girl ever accused you of anything?"

"Of being an asshole? A disgusting pig? A couple times, yeah. Of being a rapist? No. But I dunno. You tell me, you have some distance. Has anyone ever said anything?"

"Everyone says stuff, Raph—"

"Okay, so people talk."

"Well, look, there's nothing concrete. Nothing I know of. I don't have any name or situation—"

"Still, people say stuff."

He'll look at you, his face graver, more serious. "Well, like, yeah, they do," he'll say.

You'll get up, pace around. Then lose your temper—"What do you know about how people fuck? You've been with Sophie since, like, grade ten, right?"

"Raph, this is an opportunity."

"An *opportunity*?"

"If ever anyone should...I just want us to be prepared."

"Prepared?"

"My lawyer's on her way over."

"A lawyer? Why a lawyer?"

"Purely as a preventive measure."

"But I have my meeting at two."

"I cancelled it."

"I'm the boss, Thom. Not you."

"I know. But right now I think you ought to listen to me."

You'll give in to the urge to turn your phone back on. Texts have flooded in from André, Max Lap, and others. Sam has left you a voice mail, plus he's sent a slew of texts:

Raph I guess you've seen it

The email?

I'm freaking

Fuck

Who's the cunt who wrote that?

They can't do that

They're just throwing out names

Any schoolkid can do that

I don't get it man

It's fucked

We gotta talk man

Please call me

Raph?

Raph call me

Please

"I JUST WANT TO WARN YOU IT WON'T BE PLEASANT. BUT I need you to be completely transparent with me. Okay?"

"Okay."

The lawyer will arrive a half-hour into your meeting with Thomas. She'll have you sign several documents after describing and explaining them in detail, though understanding what she says is too much of an effort for you. You'll just smile stupidly whenever she speaks to you. You'll have trouble focusing because you keep making eye contact with Thomas's assistant on the other side of the window into the office. She'll seem to be following the events with morbid curiosity.

The lawyer will be attractive in a way you're not really used to. You don't move in the same circles as professional women with conservative haircuts and well-pressed suits. You interact with them very rarely—in fact, never.

At any other time, in any other context, you'd probably try to hold her gaze a little, make her laugh by breaking the rules for the kind of situation you're in. However, she's completely neutralized your only power by forcing you to be serious. You're nothing when you're forced to be serious.

"I'll need us to draw up a list of everyone you've had contact with who might potentially accuse you of one of the acts mentioned in the email."

"Wouldn't it be better if I did this with a man?" you'll ask.

"Why?" she'll say.

You'll consider being honest with her, saying it'd be easier to admit to a man that you've been a pig, but you'll remember that people seldom get out of these situations by being honest.

After a pause, she'll say, "Let me reassure you that you're protected by attorney-client privilege."

You won't feel protected.

"Okay," you'll say. "So, like, every girl ever?"

"Every girl with whom you might have possibly had the kind of interaction described in the email."

Thomas will crack his neck, the sound so loud in the conference room that you'll worry about his spinal cord.

"That's a lot of girls," you'll say seriously to the lawyer. In any other context, you'd speak in a completely different tone. In any other context, you'd brag. You'd be a winner.

"We'll list as many as possible. We need to take inventory— as complete an inventory as circumstances allow."

"The circumstances being what?" you'll ask.

"How well you remember," the lawyer will reply with a smile.

You'll take a ragged breath. "Where do we begin?" you'll say.

"Has anyone ever come to you and accused you of committing any of these acts?"

"No, never."

"Okay, we'll go over the acts one by one. Just to see if they ring any bells."

"Alright."

"Sexual assault. Offhand does any situation come to mind?"

"No, I don't think so. But..."

Different girls will come to mind, the scenes playing out like you're fast-forwarding a film. A girl in your improv troupe in cégep: you kissed her, convinced she wanted you to, but then she slapped you in the face. A girl from the comedy school: she said in bed that she liked it rough, but when you called her a little whore during sex she began crying and wouldn't stop even after you apologized profusely. The girls you slept with the first year after our breakup: every one of them was way too drunk to give informed consent.

"For sexual assault," you'll say, "does the assault have to be conscious on my part?"

"No, not at all."

"Well, then, that means I might've assaulted all the girls I've slept with."

"No, it doesn't," Thomas will say.

You'll go teary-eyed. Thomas's assistant will be staring at you through the window.

"Well, yeah," you'll insist. "I mean, it's not like I get off on forcing girls to— But did I sit down with everyone I slept with to talk about what we both wanted? Like I never did that even once. In retrospect, it definitely seems—"

Thomas will lay a hand on your forearm. "Let's just focus on obvious incidents, Raph," he'll say.

The lawyer will look at Thomas, who'll signal for her to go on. "Grooming?" she'll say.

"Meaning, like, manipulating really young girls?"

"It's open to interpretation, but yes."

"No, I think the biggest age difference I've had with a girl is, like, five years younger. But she wasn't a minor."

"Good," the lawyer will say, sounding almost maternal.

Though you try to remain civil, you'll clearly look ticked off. It'll annoy you that she gets to judge your behaviour as good or bad.

Seeing your reaction, she'll stammer, "Sorry, I, um, I didn't mean—"

"It's alright," you'll say.

"No worries," Thomas will say.

"I'm not here to pass judgment. I want that to be clear. I'm just gathering facts. When I said 'good' in this context, it was just a verbal tic."

You'll look at her, poker-faced for a half second, then say, "Good."

She'll let out a laugh, bringing the tension down a notch. She'll peer at her screen again, clear her throat, then take on a more serious tone. "Soliciting nude photos?" she'll say.

"Yeah, yeah. But, like, in a flirting situation. I mean, everybody does it, exchange nudes. Right?"

Thomas will turn away, look outside, rub his hands nervously on his thighs. The lawyer will type something on her laptop.

"Sending unsolicited nude photos?"

"No. Again, I sent nudes, but only as part of an exchange."

"Okay."

"Sexual harassment?"

"God, I dunno. It's a broad term. But, like, I don't think so, no. I mean, I don't think I've ever grabbed a girl's breasts or butt totally without warning."

"Physical harassment?"

"I don't think so."

"Exposing your genitals?"

"Uh, yeah."

A moment of tension. Thomas will purse his lips.

"But as a joke. Like, just with the guys." You'll turn to Thomas and say, "Even you did it, Thom."

He'll glance uneasily at the lawyer, then turn back to you, looking like he wants you to zip it.

You'll explain to the lawyer: "Thomas, Max Lap, Sam, and

me, we had this inside joke at school. Back then, Thomas was in our class since he was studying comedy too. So anyway, when me and the guys were in the green room, if one of us was sitting down, someone else would come up behind him and lay his dick on the guy's shoulder. I admit it wasn't high comedy, but it was still a joke."

"Did you do it in front of girls?"

"Well, we had two girls in our class, so yeah."

"It's true that Elena hated when we'd take our dicks out," Thomas will say.

"Oh, for chrissake, come on," you'll say. "Elena has a sense of humour."

Thomas will look at you without saying anything, like he's seeing his entire youth pass before his eyes.

The lawyer will pause a moment, stare at you both, then go on. "Persistent unwanted online contact?"

"Hmm...I really don't think so."

"Have you ever covered up any of these acts?"

"Meaning what exactly?"

"Have you ever covered up for friends or acquaintances who behaved this way?"

"Maybe. I mean, I *have* covered for friends cheating on their girlfriends."

Decisions are made in an instant. In a flash, the blink of an eye, a split second, we calculate the consequences and make a choice.

"There's also Sam, though," you'll say.

"Sam?" the lawyer will ask, looking up from her screen.

"Samuel Bouvier."

There are times when we know we should feel guilty. Times when we know we're being petty. But it feels so good.

"I mean, I've never covered for him, not really, not in the

sense of making a pact to hide a dead body. Nothing like that. But, y'know, Sam does have a reputation."

It'll feel *so* good.

"A reputation?" the lawyer will ask, her guard up.

"Sam sleeps around a lot. And, y'know, he has a reputation for sometimes being..."

"Being what?"

"I dunno, being rough. Basically, though, I don't really know since me and him don't talk much about sex. But people do say stuff. I could maybe, I dunno, be accused of being his friend and turning a blind eye."

"But is there an incident where you deliberately hid things? Told a girl to keep quiet? Lied to cover up something he'd done?"

"No, not really. But I admit I sometimes wonder if somebody might blame me for not raising a red flag. If you jump into a lake and some guy watches you knowing the lake's teeming with piranhas, can you blame him because he didn't warn you?"

Thomas's phone will vibrate, knocking hard against the glass table. Seeing the screen, he'll frown but still answer.

"Hello?" He'll glance at you, give you a look of death. "No. No can do," he'll say. "Unfortunately, no. Nope. No."

He'll set his phone face down on the table, force a smile. The lawyer will also smile uneasily.

"Who was it?" you'll ask.

"No one."

"Who was it, Thom?"

"Raph."

"Thom, I'm the boss. Me."

He'll sigh, rub his face. "The guy from *La Presse* who wrote that great article on you and Sam," he'll say. "Gabriel

Doré-Lapierre."

"What'd he want?"

"He... Oh, Raph, really, it's not a good idea."

"What?"

"He wants to talk to you."

"About what?"

"I'd advise against it," the lawyer will say.

Thomas will nod and point to the woman. "Listen to her," he'll say.

"THANKS FOR TAKING TIME TO MEET WITH ME," THE reporter will say. He suggested a phone interview, but you insisted on meeting in person. You're nothing without a live audience.

He's come to Thomas's office. Thomas has given you the conference room. He originally flipped out about the interview, but you argued you knew what you were doing and could set things right. Thomas wasn't convinced.

"It's the least I could do," you'll tell the reporter.

Reporters, especially arts reporters, will always fascinate you. It's part of their job description to be up-to-date on the latest trends, attuned to current events, but Gabriel Doré-Lapierre, like many of his peers, will look like a small-town accountant. He'll be socially awkward but have a nice face.

"It must be weird for you right now," he'll say.

"That's one way of putting it."

"Congrats on Samuel's gala by the way. You were excellent."

"Thanks."

"It's pretty strange to go from a feature interview with the two of you to...this."

This. He'll be stalling. You can't tell if it's because you intimidate him, if he's scared to jump right in, or if he's about to back you into a corner.

You'll just smile at the guy. Behind him is the window into the office. Thomas will walk by, looking as white as a ghost.

"I admit I'd rather be talking to you about your next show

than about this other thing."

"We can talk about my new show another time."

He'll give you a strained smile, then take a notebook out of his bag and lay his phone on the table.

"I wanted to talk to you mostly to corroborate certain information. Just to make sure the facts add up before we go to press."

"Okay, but aren't you afraid my comments will be biased?"

"Well, that's why I try to vary my sources. You ready to start?"

He'll tap the red Dictaphone button on his cell.

"Okay, we're recording."

Sound waves will appear on the screen of his phone, and his tone will become just a bit more formal.

"Can you tell me about your relationship with Samuel Bouvier?"

"We were in the same class at the comedy school."

"Would you say he was a friend?"

"Yeah, I would."

"You continued seeing each other after you graduated, right?"

"Yeah, we worked together a lot and crossed paths professionally. And he was a close friend. He is. Well, I..."

The reporter will give you a sympathetic look.

"But we've seen each other less in the past year."

"Why's that?"

"Oh, y'know, we've both been swamped with work. And I quit drinking, so I don't go out much anymore."

"Did you guys party together a lot?"

You'll hold back a little laugh. "Yeah, well, that's all part of the game."

"Meaning what?"

"That we got trashed a lot. I mean, stand-up is a club scene, so..."

"How much were you drinking?"

"Tons. Look, no comic I know goes onstage sober."

"Was it just booze?"

"Sam had a cocaine problem."

"Did you stop drinking for a particular reason?"

"Oh, y'know, the usual reasons. To lose weight. That kind of thing."

Your gaze will drift to one of the Oliviers you left on Thomas's trophy shelf.

"How would you describe Sam after he has a couple drinks?"

"Hmm. He has no filters, I'd say."

"Okay. So did his behaviour become problematic at all when he was drinking?"

"Define 'problematic,'" you'll say, getting cocky. It'll be like when you zero in on somebody in the audience to make everyone else laugh. But, this time, it'll be trickier because there's no one around to laugh. Still, the reporter will smile.

"Did Sam tend to be insistent, with girls?"

Your eyes will shift to the window. "Take a guy who was probably a bit of a reject in high school," you'll say. "What if, all of a sudden, thousands of people start telling him he's God's gift? Eventually, the dude may come to think he's frigging invincible."

"Did you witness any specific incidents that make you say that?"

"Apparently, Forand sent hush money to some of his clients' victims."

"Forand, Samuel Bouvier's manager?"

"Yeah."

"Do you have proof of that?"

"*I* don't, but there's a girl named Laurie Blais who used to work as Forand's assistant. Contact her and she can confirm it for sure. Apparently, she was asked to send money orders to these girls."

You'll watch him anxiously scrawling notes as he tries to keep up with you. Before he even finishes, you'll add, "Have you talked to a girl named Soleil?"

Caught off guard, he'll look down at his notes, then back up at you. "I, um, yeah," he'll say.

He'll flip back through his notebook, looking for earlier notes he's taken down. "That's one of the things I wanted to verify with you," he'll say. "That girl...Soleil Dupras...she said you were there the night she met Sam."

"Yeah, me and Sam were on the bill at Le Terminal that night."

"So what do you know about what happened between them?"

"Nothing, basically, that's the thing. I mean, if I'd *really* known something had gone down, I might've, like, done something. Know what I mean?"

"Yeah, yeah. But can we start from the beginning? Maybe just tell me—"

"Well, y'know, I just drove them to Sam's place. I don't know anything else. Except maybe, except..."

The guy will watch you take your phone out of your pocket, search through your old voice mails. You'll set your phone down on the table between the two of you, just beside his phone.

"Except maybe this."

"What's this?"

Your phone's speaker will spit out the awful crackling

sound of someone breathing frantically into the microphone. The breathing will move away from the mic, slow down. Sobs will be heard, then this: "Why didn't you tell me your friend was a psycho?"

The reporter will just stare at you. "Do you always save your messages for this long?" he'll ask.

"Always. I never forget a thing."

YOU'LL POST A STORY ON THE MORNING THE NEWSPAPER article comes out. Your post will first go through Thomas, the lawyer, and a public-relations firm. Never will something you've written be so carefully edited, vetted, calculated.

Hi. Like everybody else, I just read the article in La Presse *about Samuel Bouvier. Like everybody else, I'm totally shocked. I won't be collaborating with Samuel on any more projects. I want to apologize to all of his alleged victims. Samuel was my friend, and maybe I should've asked more questions and confronted him. Not many people dare speak up, which is maybe part of the problem. Collectively, we need to stop looking away when we see problem behaviour. Stay strong. I believe you.*

You'll have over a hundred thousand followers by this point. You'll be glad I pushed you to develop your web content.

I'VE GOT NON-ALCOHOLIC BEER. KOMBUCHA TOO.
Elena will be bending over in front of the fridge, back slightly arched, ass sticking out. You'll feel uneasy looking at her, so you stare at the floor instead.

"Are you crazy?" you'll say. "Give me a real beer."

"I thought you'd quit."

"That was a lifetime ago."

She'll take out two tallboys of double IPA, nudge the fridge door closed with her butt, hand you a beer. "Cheers," she'll say.

You'll pull the tab, then knock your can against hers. Take a moment to check out the acoustic panels on the walls, the fake plants in the entrance. The studio will look rundown, the concrete floor and walls flaking. Like some workshop from another era.

Elena will catch you eyeing the place. "Ideally, we'd be doing this in my basement, but I'm too lazy and cheap to buy the gear. This is André's set-up. He does his own podcast here and also rents the place out."

"It's good he's switching careers."

Elena will throw you a look, both appalled and satisfied. "Save that for when we're recording," she'll say.

"I'd never say that on tape. I adore André."

"But you want him switching careers."

"Awesome dude. Crap comedian."

She'll nod, amused, then point to your chair at the table in the studio. She'll sit on the other side, two mics between you.

"I'm happy to see you," she'll say. "It's been a while."

"What can I say? Busy with work."

You really like Elena, you'll always really like her. You find her comforting. You know each other well, can appreciate each other. There's enough distance between you guys to avoid any bad blood.

"Glad to know you haven't gotten too big to appear on my humble podcast."

"You know I can never say no to you. And I think it's a super innovative concept, a podcast with two comedians drinking beer and talking shit."

"There's a twist—two comedians drinking beer and talking shit, but one's a *woman*. Unprecedented."

Elena will turn to the laptop beside her, peer at the screen a bit, then turn back to you. "We're recording," she'll say. Her voice will go up an octave and get bubblier. "How are you doing, Raph?"

"Well, that's a loaded question," you'll say.

Elena will lift her can to you. You'll do likewise. After a pause, she'll say in confidence to her listeners, "The silence you just heard was the sound of two people stuck in quicksand."

"Where shall we start, Elena?"

"Maybe the real question is, where will it all end?"

You'll emit a grave *hmm*.

She'll go on: "First of all, I invited you here because I miss you and it's been ages since we've seen each other."

"And second of all," you'll add, "what the fuck is going on?"

She'll let out a laugh. You'll be proud of your joke. You know what sets Elena off. You know how to make her laugh and you'll continue to make her laugh.

"In case you don't know this, me and Raph went to the

comedy school together with Sam Bouvier. So...let's just say life's been interesting this past month."

"'Interesting'? Why so politically correct all of a sudden, Elena?"

"Okay, okay." She'll look you defiantly in the eye. "It's been a shitshow. Better? But there are some glimmers of hope, and I'd like to focus on those too."

"Like what?"

"Like the fact that we have allies. For example, people like you. Y'know, it's super admirable the way you've really tried to look at the situation from every angle. I feel like you've handled it all pretty courageously."

"Yeah, but obviously, in hindsight, I look at what happened and think, Could I have stepped in sooner? Did I overlook stuff I shouldn't have?"

"But if you go down that road, it's never-ending. Us girls second-guess ourselves too. Y'know, I sometimes think I was pretty stupid not to have set boundaries with guys. So then to get involved in somebody else's drama? Obviously we're not always keen to."

"Yeah, you're right."

"And I admit I'm sick of explaining to idiots online that it's not okay to message me dick pics. Or having to tell guys to stop touching my ass. So if just *once* occasionally a guy takes the initiative to put his foot down and say enough's enough, it gives me a little break. So you'll get no complaints from me."

She'll take a sip of her beer, then glance out the window, which looks out over the mountain and the downtown lights, everything cloaked in a cloudy haze.

"I thought of something this week," you'll say. "I realized I was goddamn lucky to spend high school getting called a fag."

She'll utter a little *ohhh* in sympathy.

"I figure it may have saved me a bit from, y'know, that whole culture. Because it starts young, like in the locker room with your hockey team."

"Improv teams have their own macho culture too, right?" You'll both laugh—a forced laugh.

"I'm suddenly remembering the names of all of these guys," Elena will say.

The conversation will go on like that for quite a while. Elena has lots of good qualities, but don't ask her to make a long story short. You'll get through the interview playing the nice guy who's disappointed in his friend and siding with the women. And it'll work. It'll work like a charm.

When Elena stops recording, you'll feel like you've run a marathon.

"Was it alright?" you'll ask her.

"It was great, Raph. With you, it's always great."

"Cool. I wasn't sure if you wanted something more..." You'll shake your head, unable to finish your sentence, then try again: "I wasn't sure what you wanted for your show, like, if you wanted me to be remorseful, or on the defensive, or just chill—"

Elena will shake her head too. "No, I just wanted to hear what you had to say."

You'll gather your bag, hurry to leave, stressed out, tense.

"Heading off already?" Elena will ask.

"Yeah, I'm shooting early tomorrow."

"Well, have a nice night then."

Elena will kiss you on the cheek. You'll wonder if there was any possibility of you guys sleeping together again. You'll step away from her, open the door. Before you leave, you'll turn back to her. "You never had any moments with me," you'll ask, "when you thought, like, Oh, that was really kinda awful?"

She'll pause before answering, long enough that you feel forced to look her in the eye. "No," she'll finally say. "But I'm not every girl you've ever slept with, Raph."

THE SONG "ADIEU" BY CŒUR DE PIRATE WILL BE PLAYING when you walk out. You'll take a seat on the set of the talk show. It'll be the start of the Beaujolais Nouveau season, so you'll be offered a glass. "I don't drink," you'll say politely. "But thanks anyway."

Of course, you'll still drink, just never in public. The rider for your tour will even specify that you don't want any alcohol in the green-room fridge. Instead, you'll travel with a flask, which is more discreet. Your image will be of a reformed party boy, which people will love. It'll fit the theme of your second show. You'll sell the idea of a more mature guy, who's been through hell and come out the other side.

"Raphaël Massicotte," the talk show's host, Guy A. Lepage, will say, "in two weeks, you'll present the media premiere of a brand new one-man show called *Sick*. This time around, you're promising us a darker, more introspective, more biting form of comedy. I actually saw a pretty shocking bit where you talk rather bluntly about how hard it is to speak about suicide to a friend with mental health issues. So are you here to make us laugh or make us cry?"

A tinkling of laughter from the audience.

"Well, y'know, is there any place where it's more liberating to laugh than at a funeral?"

Lepage's face will break into a grin.

"With this show, I have fun being deliberately darker and acting a bit crueller, like how we are when we're fourteen years old but are afraid to be once we're adults."

"Calling the show 'mature' is false advertising then? Will you be doing dead-baby jokes?"

Big laughs from the audience. Another guest, Quebec's justice minister, will be sitting across from you on the set. He'll smile in spite of himself, then take a swig of his wine.

"Anything goes," you'll say, "as long as I sell some tickets."

"Raphaël, you've become hugely successful since the launch of your first show," Lepage will say. "You won three Oliviers the very first year you were nominated. You're everywhere now. We see you on TV, we hear you on the radio, you're still active on your YouTube page where we first discovered you. How are you handling the pressure of a second show?"

"Oh, very badly," you'll say. "My plan tonight is to lower your expectations."

A giggle from the singer Marie-Mai, who's seated beside you.

"But seriously, it'd be dishonest of me to bitch about the pressure of my second show. Am I sweating bullets? You bet. Would I rather that people not wanna see my new show because they hated the first? Definitely not. So, look, I'm doing my best, and if you guys don't like the show, give me your address and I'll personally go to your house and throw eggs at your windows."

Hysterical laughter from the audience.

"Raphaël, you were recently quoted in an article by Gabriel Doré-Lapierre in *La Presse* that addressed the sexual misconduct allegations against Samuel Bouvier."

"Yeah," you'll say, then purse your lips.

"The article alleges that Samuel Bouvier behaved inappropriately on several occasions and even committed sexual assault and that his talent agency paid hush money to his victims. You're quoted as saying you weren't surprised by the allegations, but you were shocked nonetheless. How can someone be shocked without being surprised?"

You'll take a deep breath.

"Rumours are funny. I mean, we hear so many different things. But when the information comes from the friend of a friend of a friend, what are we supposed to do? Should we automatically sever ties with someone we've heard bad things about? There's no instruction manual for these situations. What I can tell you, though, is that as soon as I *saw* this horrible behaviour with my own eyes, I cut Sam off."

A pause. Lepage will open his mouth to speak, but you'll jump back in: "I took no joy in doing this, I can assure you. Sam was a friend of mine, someone I'd known for a long time. You don't drop a friend like that for the hell of it. In the end, though, I think the industry has maybe been too permissive with a lot of people for a variety of reasons: because the public loves a certain comedian, because the guy's a cash cow, because we don't wanna believe the accusers. And I've probably been guilty of that myself and should've cut Sam off way sooner. And I feel like those who still work with him, who still validate his work, have some serious questions to ask themselves. Because, in some ways, working with him means encouraging that kind of behaviour."

As you say this, you'll picture me sitting in front of my TV. This image will warm your heart.

IT'LL BE LATE. YOU'VE JUST COME BACK FROM SAINT-Hyacinthe. It rained the whole drive back on Highway 20. You were afraid a couple times that you'd nod off behind the wheel.

The show went well. Your new show will always go well no matter where you perform it.

Your mind will be a blank. In the past few months, you've managed to live in a world that's smooth, spotless, endlessly beige in all directions. You'll float like you're in a thick amniotic fluid of ennui. A world without danger, surprise, drama. A world you can live in without feeling a thing.

It'll still be raining hard as you walk up to the entrance to your building. A homeless guy in a dripping raincoat will be standing in the lobby in front of the security guard's desk. Your neighbourhood will attract a lot of homeless people, but they won't really bother you. Since they don't have TV, it'll be easier for you to share space with them. They'll be less annoying than the ladies who accost you at the grocery store to make some comment they think is funny and smart but is neither. A way for them to say, "I know you exist, and by letting you know, I feel a bit like I exist too."

You'll politely ignore the guy, head to the elevator. The security guard will get up from his desk and say, "You've got a friend waiting for you, Mr. Massicotte. I figured I wouldn't make a colleague of yours stand outside in this weather."

You'll turn. The homeless guy will lower his hood. It'll be Sam. Or an approximation of Sam. A rough sketch of Sam with sad-dog eyes. You'll stand there saying nothing, just staring at this ghostly figure. You'll wonder if he's armed. You'll feel bad for wondering, then decide that no, the idea's not so far-fetched. You'll glance around to see if anyone else is there. You'll calculate the likelihood that you'll run into a neighbour in your building and that the person will recognize both of you. The likelihood that this neighbour will then blab, that word will spread, that you'll become guilty by association. The chances will seem pretty slim to you.

"Can we talk?" Sam will say.

You'll just nod, turn on your heel, walk toward the elevator. The security guard will watch you guys go, intrigued by Sam. You'll wonder if it's possible he's never heard or read anything about Sam. You'll wonder if he even gives a shit.

The elevator doors will slide open. You'll glance around one last time before you enter. Sam will follow. Once the doors close, he'll say, "I know I look like a psycho right now. It's just..." A loud sniff. His jaw will tremble. The elevator hum will be comforting since it fills the few seconds of silence.

"Nobody will talk to me anymore," Sam will say. "Nobody replies to my texts. It's like I'm dead to everyone. I'm just...I'm so fucking lonely, man. It's nice of you to let me come up."

You'll miss the perfect stasis that Sam has pulled you out of.

"How long were you waiting in the lobby?"

"I dunno. My phone died. An hour? An hour and a half?"

When the elevator doors open, you'll instinctively glance around before heading down the corridor. Like you're committing a crime. You'll walk quickly, almost jog. Like you want to get away from Sam. Like by moving fast, you're shouting, "I don't know this guy!"

You'll feel your blood pressure come down once you walk

through the door of your apartment.

You'll put your bag and keys down. Turn the lights on.

"Nice place," Sam will say.

"Yeah, well, it's not like I built it myself."

"It looks very adult."

"Eventually you get fed up with sleeping on a mattress on the floor and eating out of plastic dishes from Value Village."

"Yeah."

"And it's a nice building. A super location. The view's great. I really like it here."

There'll be no underground parking, though. If there was, you wouldn't have gone through the lobby. You wouldn't have run into Sam.

"I gotta take some time to furnish the place a bit more. You know how it is with work. It's like when I have time off, the last thing on my mind is interior decorating."

Sam will grunt in agreement.

"Are you still in Rosemont?" you'll ask.

"No, no, I sold the place."

You'll wait for him to explain, maybe to make some comment about real estate, like "The bidding wars are crazy nowadays," something that lets you extend your truce and continue with the small talk. You spent a good part of your life shunning small talk, only to discover later that it actually helps you survive, lets you avoid getting too serious. Without small talk, you'd have to go deeper. Or worse—keep quiet. No way can you keep quiet. Your whole career's built on you talking.

But Sam won't help you here. "It's the legal fees," he'll say. "They bled me dry, and I had no money coming in, so..."

"Oh, I see."

"No, I don't think you do."

It won't seem like an attack. It'll sound like a fact.

After a lull, you'll say nervously, "You can take your coat off, y'know."

"Yeah, okay," he'll say but keep it on.

"Want a beer?"

"No, no. I...I just got out of rehab. So..."

Of course you've heard rumours about this. You never ask questions about Sam, never deliberately try to find anything out, but whenever his name comes up, particularly his troubles, you'll revel in the schadenfreude.

"Oh, yeah, okay," you'll say. "I feel you."

"Ever been in rehab?"

"No, but I did quit drinking for a year, remember?"

"Oh, yeah."

"I never felt so lousy in all my life. Do not do it."

You'll go to your fridge, take out an IPA. The tallboy will make a loud fizz as you pull the tab. You'll take a big sip.

"I don't have anything good without alcohol. Want a glass of water?"

"No, it's okay."

Another lull.

"I became so boring when I was sober," you'll say. "I was always so self-conscious."

"Yeah, same."

"I'd like to tell you it'll eventually get better, but that'd be a big lie. How long are you quitting for?"

"It's supposed to be for life."

"Oh."

"Yeah."

You'll notice that he's lost weight, but not in a good way. You'll feel forced to make conversation. "Seen anyone from school lately?"

"No, people aren't being too chummy anymore."

"Hmm, I see," you'll say. "Max Lap's career's on the rise. He's really kicked it up a notch."

Another long silence. You can't stand it. You'll flounder around, then say, "He's gonna be a dad, y'know."

"Oh, really?"

"Yeah."

Another lull.

"I did a show tonight."

"Where were you?"

"Saint-Hyacinthe."

"Did you kill?"

"Yeah."

"Yeah, gigs in Saint-Hyacinthe often go great, right?"

"Yeah, and the show's pretty solid now. The reviews were good for the premiere. We're almost sold out already."

"Cool. Very cool. I'm working on some new material too."

"Oh, really?"

You'll try to hide your contempt. Sam will be worse off than you thought. He has to be out of his mind to think he can go back onstage.

"Yeah, like a comeback show. I think people are ready for that. Y'know, hear my side of the story. Clear the air. Sort of make amends."

A comeback, you'll think. A comeback just a few months after his fall. You'll swallow the urge to burst his bubble.

"Oh, yeah. Cool. That must be keeping you busy."

"Yeah."

You'll finally give in and say, "So...why'd you wanna see me?"

"No reason."

"No reason?"

"No."

"Just to talk?" you'll say. "A Wednesday at midnight. In the rain."

"You're not much for texting and don't answer my calls. I've invited you to go for a beer like a hundred times, and you've never gotten back to me."

"You know what it's like. I'm busy, man. Swamped with work."

"Everybody says that."

"Well, everybody works."

"We used to see each other before. Even with work."

You'll try to lighten the mood with a joke. "Y'know, it was super creepy of you to sneak into my building like that."

He'll move for the first time since he arrived. He'll come toward you, lean against the corner of the kitchen counter. He'll totally ignore your attempt at humour.

"I haven't seen anyone in two months, not counting rehab or the people I pay, like my shrink, my doctor, the guy who does my groceries, the deliverymen. No one else."

"You don't see..."

"Who?"

"Laurie?"

"Why would I see Laurie?"

"I dunno. Weren't you working together on your show?"

"Yeah, well...that's dead. Just like everything else."

"Oh, okay."

"So you get why I'm going a bit crazy, all alone at home?"

"Uh-huh. But, you know..."

"What?"

"You do get that certain people might not wanna see you. For plenty of valid reasons."

"Oh, come on. I'm not radioactive."

"No, but it'd probably be easier if it *was* only that. At least there are special suits to wear."

He'll just stare into space, like he's lost inside his own head. To snap him out of it, you'll ask, "How was rehab?"

"Honestly?"

"Yeah."

"Absolute hell."

"That's what everybody says, right?"

"If I'd wanted to wake up at six in the morning and get yelled at for not making my bed, I would've joined the army."

"It's that bad?"

"And when I'm sober, I'm not funny or fun. I'm pathetic and bland and stupid. I annoy everyone, and everything annoys me. They put you in rehab and say, 'Hey, don't freak. It's tough, but it's temporary.' Then you get out and they're like, 'Good luck, dude, it'll actually be like this for the rest of your life.' And you're supposed to have figured all your shit out."

"I feel you."

"No, I don't think you do, but...it doesn't matter. I mean, I don't even know if I can still work, man. When I try to come up with material, it's like...like I've been reprogrammed. I'm the fucking dullest guy around now."

"Is that why you're here?"

"What?"

"Rehab. Like don't they make you go see people after you get out?"

"No, no."

"So you can, like, apologize to them and stuff?"

"God, no, it's not that kind of place. It's not New Agey."

"Oh, okay."

"And why would I apologize?"

"Huh?"

"Why would I come here to apologize to you?"

Another lull. You'll wonder if you've tripped up, entered a danger zone. You'll shrug. "I dunno," you'll say. "I...I was just, like, speculating."

"I didn't do anything to you. And, y'know, I didn't do anything to anyone else either."

"I don't know about that, Sam."

"What do you mean?"

"Forget it. It's just—"

"No, what?"

"Sam, come on. Don't go burying your head in the sand."

"What?" he'll say, teeth clenched.

"This whole thing wasn't, like, fake news. I mean, shit did happen."

"How would you know?" Sam will say sharply.

You'll concede that point. "I wouldn't, I guess. I wasn't in the bedroom with you."

"Are you fucking serious?" he'll say, louder now. He'll spit when he speaks, like he always does onstage. "What bedroom are you talking about?"

You'll try to calm him down. "I didn't mean anything by that—"

"Can you try showing just a bit of empathy, for fuck sake? Your name could've ended up so easily on that list too."

You'll look him directly in the eye to show his grace period's up.

He'll look away, his spine straighter, the colour back in his cheeks. He'll speak faster now. He'll become the old Sam—the guy with a little fire in his belly who gets worked up when things, or usually people, piss him off.

"Don't pretend you're a fucking saint, Raph. Jesus Christ!

You just got lucky. You've fucked how many girls since I met you? Statistically, it's almost certain that one night things got out of hand and a girl felt you went too far too fast. The only difference probably is that that girl didn't have such a big fucking mouth."

"Dude, stop."

He'll take a breath to calm down but have trouble sucking in air. Before he can breathe normally, words will tumble out of his mouth. "You didn't need to kick a guy when he was down, y'know." He'll almost seem to be choking, like he's struggling to stay afloat in a lake while his lungs fill with water. Each breath will now be ragged, painful.

"I didn't kick—"

"Dude, you were like, 'I believe you' and 'Let's take out the trash.' Overnight, a guy who used to tell cunt jokes becomes the number-one feminist ally in Quebec."

"You weren't the only one accused."

"And that goddamn article in the paper. You fucking sold me out!"

"I just told him what I knew—"

"What you *assumed*—"

"And what everybody knew, by the way—"

"Dude, I...I thought you were my friend," he'll say, his voice quavering. "Like...like nobody put a gun to your head and told you to pick a side."

"Not literally, no. But, I mean, you saw what the climate was like..."

"No, I didn't, man. I swore off the news pretty damn fast."

"Well, keeping quiet was seen as supporting the men. So I...I just did what I was told to do to stay out of trouble."

He'll shake his head frantically awhile, pant like a dog. He'll be leaning against the counter, his hair in his face. A string of drool will drop from his mouth to the floor. He'll look totally deranged. "To stay out of trouble," he'll say. "To stay out of fucking trouble."

He'll slide down the side of the counter till he's sitting on the floor. He'll be crying now. "It wasn't a good idea to come here," he'll say softly.

"No, it wasn't. I told you."

You won't be able to go near him. You'll just stare at the floor and hope he disappears magically into thin air.

Through his sobs, he'll mutter, "Raph?"

He'll sound pleading, so you'll feel forced to look at him.

"Was it just because of Laurie?" he'll say.

"What?"

"Did you do it out of revenge?"

"No, man. You're being crazy."

"*I'm* the crazy one?"

Sam will know you well enough to know how to use the past to his advantage. He'll know how to bring you down with four words, using just the right intonation and tilt of his head, a combination that conjures up a notion, a place, a time, a whole story, the story of me and you. He'll be reminding you that you took way too long to get over me—if you ever really did. Reminding you that if anyone's weak, it's you, not him, and that if anyone would resort to ruining a person's life out of the simple base desire for revenge, it's also you. Reminding you that the crazy one will always be you. Not him.

That's what you'll hear when Sam says, "*I'm* the crazy one?" It may not be what he means, but it'll be what you hear. And you'll realize that maybe you wouldn't have heard it if you didn't at least agree somewhat that it's true.

"They should've taken you down too."

"That way, you'd feel less alone, with us in the same boat?"

"No, that way, it'd be more fair."

"I didn't fuck minors, Sam."

He'll struggle to his feet, adjust his raincoat, then head to your front door. As he opens it, he'll say, "I just wanna say you had the chance to make someone feel a little less shitty tonight, but you fucking blew it."

After Sam slams the door, you'll listen to his footsteps go down your carpeted corridor. You'll realize you've just lost the person in this world who knows you best. And you'll tell yourself it's maybe a good thing. It's easier to sail through life when there's no one around who knows exactly where all your weak spots are.

IN SIX YEARS AND A FEW MONTHS, IN THE SPRING, IN April, on April 20th to be exact, you and me will see each other for the last time. It'll be a miracle, in fact, that we never crossed paths earlier. After all, Quebec is small, and our lives, yours and mine, were so intertwined for a while. It's hard to believe something that was once fused together can be split apart. But it can be. After this date, we'll never see each other again. Never. And it's not even because we'll die young. No, we'll both die old, even though you hoped to join the 27 Club.

We'll meet again completely by chance, if there's such a thing as chance.

It'll happen at the airport. You'll be coming back from Sept-Îles, where you performed. You'll have to fly back because Thomas has booked you on a game show the day after your gig. You'll have tens of thousands of tickets to sell every year, so you'll take all the exposure you can get. You can't afford to be picky.

You'll be hurrying to the exit, a backpack on your back, your phone to your ear, busy pretending you're talking to someone so you can avoid being accosted by annoying fans who'd lay a hand on your shoulder without asking permission, then quote out of context some joke you told once back in 2013 at a comedy night in Longueuil, because they think it's a fun way to start a conversation, forcing you then to be nice and to fake interest in people who are your bread and butter, people you need in order to earn a living and simply exist, but people you have trouble interacting with unless they number in the hundreds and you get to stand onstage with spotlights on you. By this time, you'll have everything you ever wanted, and you'll still find reason to whine. But not as much as when I broke up with you.

When you pass the baggage carousel, you'll throw a slightly scornful look at the plebeians waiting there for the giant suitcases they lugged along for their five measly days in Puerto Vallarta, and you'll congratulate yourself on being one of the few geniuses who know how to travel smart and can make do with a carry-on bag for the sake of efficiency.

And while you cut through the crowd, eyes on the floor, phone to your ear, exaggerating your uh-huhs to buy yourself some peace and quiet and keep other human beings at bay, one person will stand out. A face you'll recognize, though not exactly, more like a carbon copy of a carbon copy of a carbon copy, a composite sketch made from memory a hundred years after the fact. No, not a hundred—six. Six years isn't a century, but it can seem like it.

A pale, faded, dried-up carbon copy of the girl I am today. A carbon copy of me, standing there, waiting at the baggage carousel, looking tired, staring into the distance. Me, the girl who inhabited your head every day, every hour, every minute for years. Me, the real me, messy hair, no makeup. Me, unworthy of the role of nemesis that you've cast me in for so long and that no longer suits me, because despite what you imagined, I've changed, and not because of you.

Me, the girl you would've ignored in any other circumstance. That girl will now be centre frame, right in front of you, too close to avoid. A girl who'll recognize something as anonymous and trivial as your fake uh-huhs on the phone. And who'll see through your act.

You'll freeze in front of me, make a heroic effort not to

smile. You'll utter my name, but without enthusiasm, surprise, or any emotion at all. You'll say it the same way you might say, "Oh, here's the door."

"Laurie."

I won't react any more than you. You'll hope it's because I'm afraid of you, or because I'm sad, or because I have regrets and see our past flash before my eyes, or because I envy you or lust after you, or all those possibilities at once. But you can't really tell. You may have many talents, but they don't include being able to read me. For that, you'd give your right arm. Both arms, in fact.

"Raph."

I'll speak in the same monotone as you. Two gunslingers in a Mexican standoff at Montreal-Trudeau. In an ideal world, there'd be silence, the entire scene would freeze, darkness would suddenly fall over the terminal, and all the extras around us would vanish. Only our faces would remain, floating in the dark, bathed in divine light. But the reality will be much less theatrical: a big dude in hunting clothes will nudge me out of the way to gather his duffle bag and hunting bow, a mom will apologize for her baby screaming in my ear, a teenage girl will tap you on the shoulder and ask for a selfie, which you grant without looking away from me for one second.

She looks older, you'll think.

She looks older and is stooping a little, you'll think, but she's beautiful, still beautiful nonetheless. That'll piss you off big time—you can't convince yourself that I'm ugly now.

You won't know if the silence has lasted two seconds or ten minutes, but as usual, you'll feel you have to fill it. "I just got back from hunting too," you'll say.

I won't laugh. You'll take that as an affront. You're nothing if you can't get a laugh. You'll be cut down to size.

I'll just say, "Oh, really, you hunt now?"

"It was a joke."

"Oh."

You'll think I purposely didn't laugh so I could take away the weapon you always rely on to get by, to charm people, to make your mark. It'll be easier for you to imagine I stopped myself from laughing than to accept I didn't find your joke funny. Egos are like helium balloons: the bigger they get, the more fragile they become.

"No, I was doing a show. But in Sept-Îles, so it's almost like I was on a hunting trip."

"Sept-Îles."

"I have fans everywhere. The infinite power of cable TV."

Still no laugh from me. You'll feel like you're in a packed two-thousand-seat theatre and everyone's just looking at you silently and disdainfully, with their arms crossed.

"I wouldn't know," I'll just say. "I don't really watch TV anymore."

"Figure of speech," you'll say. "Social media's where it all happens nowadays anyway."

"Raph, I know."

"I didn't say that to...I mean, I know you know."

You'll almost lose patience, thinking I'm being pretty snotty. But then I'll smile, look sincere and sweet. That'll unnerve you. You'll think you were mistaken and that you came pretty close to mansplaining to me a field I know inside out. Still, you'll have no way of knowing for sure when you look at me. You can't tell what I'm feeling, which is nothing new.

"Are you back from a trip?" you'll ask.

"No, no. Well, yes and no."

A pause. You'll give me time to explain, but I won't say anything.

"So where are you coming from?"

"POV."

"POV?"

"Puvirnituq."

"Oh, up north?"

"Yeah, up north."

"Is it nice up there?"

"Yeah, it's nice." Saying this, I'll sound a bit weary. You won't know if I'm humblebragging, if I'm truly bored, or if I'm hiding something else. You've always envied my ability to say nothing, keep quiet, switch off, whereas all you can do is talk.

"What were you doing there?" you'll ask.

"I was working. I teach now."

"Oh, yeah?"

"I teach high-school French. I filled in for a teacher on maternity leave. I would've liked to finish off the year, but she came back to work."

"Oh, I didn't know you'd become a teacher."

"Yeah, well, it's not like we've stayed in touch over the years."

"Yeah. Time flies, right?"

"It sure does."

Your phone will ring—a call from Thomas. A real call this time.

"You can answer that," I'll say.

"It's not urgent," you'll say. You'll think, I've got something way more urgent at the moment.

"I didn't know you wanted to teach."

"Yeah. No, neither did I. But...yeah."

"Why a teacher?"

Why a teacher? What you really mean is this: "Why aren't you working in comedy anymore? Did you feel you were less and less in demand as time went by? Did you feel rejected? Did you feel like all your old collaborators turned against you? Was Sam's downfall the final nail in the coffin of your career? Were you humiliated when you were named in the paper as the person who mailed hush money to the victims of Forand's clients? Is that why you decided to move so far away?"

What you hope I'll answer is this: "I didn't have what it takes. I failed. I lost and you won."

"You gotta pay the rent one way or another," I'll say.

A part of you will think that I could easily cover my rent, even a mortgage, if I received residuals for your show, or for Sam's. That'll bring a smile to your face.

"And teaching lets me travel to places I never thought I'd see, so...you have to take the good with the bad."

The bad? "What do you mean?" I'll ask.

You'll believe I've slipped up, that I wanted to keep up the facade but let my guard down. In your little mind, where the gears always turn at full tilt, you'll assume that what I actually meant is that deep down I have regrets. You'll be positive that I'm looking at you, standing there in the airport with your backpack on and your straight spine, and that I'm fantasizing, maybe for the first time ever, about turning back the clock to the exact moment and place where a part of me broke away from you, and then fighting as hard as I can to hang on to you, preserve our love, keep us together, knowing my future with you would be a hundred times brighter.

It'd be a future where we'd fly back from Sept-Îles together, collect our bags while I give you notes on your performance the night before and test out the best way to word a punchline in your show. We'd climb into a taxi and head back to the apartment we'd been sharing for years in perfect harmony, a place where we'd often invite our friends, who'd consider us a true model of lasting love. The apartment would be lovely. I'd decorate it beautifully.

A few weeks later, or maybe a few months, my period would be late. I'd tell you, and we'd go buy a pregnancy test together and soon learn that we'd be parents. We'd both feel sort of dazed, thinking we weren't at all ready, but we wouldn't consider any other option but to join hands and take the leap together. You'd mention in a TV interview that we were expecting, and everyone would feel moved because you'd seem like you'd make an excellent dad.

Our baby would be born, and we'd buy a house on the South Shore. We'd end up having a second kid, because why not. We'd work together on your fourth show. It'd all go smoothly because we'd work from home and share the chores. I'd go along with you on tour, a smart idea because you could keep seeing the kids even while on the road. You'd be a great dad. Bumbling and lovable and kooky and well-meaning and generous and a good listener.

You'd wind up agreeing to host a silly game show that'd pay well. You'd secretly hate the show because it'd keep you from your goal of making unique, edgy, sophisticated comedy, but it'd allow us to buy a cottage in the Eastern Townships where we'd invite lots of friends to visit. After several good seasons, the show would be cancelled, but that wouldn't be too disappointing. I'd be far-sighted enough to have forced you to set a bunch of money aside, so we'd go off on a ten-month family trip, intending to work on your new one-man show once we got back. It'd be your first vacation in a very long time. You'd feel good. Wonderful in fact.

We'd go to Thailand. You wouldn't have gone there earlier. You wouldn't have needed to travel to take your mind off our breakup, since it never would've happened.

One evening, we'd watch the sun go down on the water, in Krabi, drinking Tiger beer as the kids play on the beach. You'd turn to me and break down in tears. I'd ask what was wrong and caress your cheek.

"I've got everything I've ever wanted," you'd say.

I'd tear up too, then kiss you.

"I don't know what I would've done," you'd add, "if you'd turned down my marriage proposal at Berghain."

"How could I have said no?"

You'll be positive that I'm picturing all that as I look at you standing in the middle of the airport, while a douchebag in a Corona cowboy hat lets out a loud burp next to you and, in the background, a couple of boomers bitch about how slow the Air Canada service is. You'll be positive that I'm picturing all that and having regrets. It'll make you feel like you've won. Winning will be all that has ever mattered.

Winning will be everything. Because the opposite would mean you'd have to admit that—even six years later, even after you've learned to get up in the morning without me being the first thing on your mind—seeing me still rattles you.

"I have to go catch my bus," I'll tell you.

Sam promised you, soon after the breakup, that years later, you and me would run into each other and you wouldn't even understand why we'd ever been together.

But all you want, that day, will be to suggest I take a taxi back with you. Go home with you. Pretend the past six years haven't happened so we can start all over again.

"Good luck," you'll say.

"With what?"

"With everything, I guess."

In the taxi, you'll stare out the window without saying much, just muttering laconic answers to the driver, who keeps gushing about the Honda commercial you appear in on TV.

Along the highway will be an enormous billboard showing a close-up of Sam's face. He'll look kinda startled, like he's just been caught doing something a little bit naughty.

SAM BOUVIER: BACK TO BASICS! TICKETS ON SALE NOW!

IT'S FOUR IN THE MORNING. THE SKY'S SLOWLY TURNING from black to royal blue. The city's at its quietest now. It feels summery, even though it's October. The perfect temperature, like when you can't even feel the air on your skin. We've been walking for at least forty minutes. You suggested a taxi, but I insisted on walking because the night's so beautiful. You liked that. You never would've taken the initiative. You aren't somebody who lives in the moment. Who changes his plans on a whim. You aren't spontaneous in your day-to-day life. You keep that for your work. You need somebody like me to coax you out of your shell.

"I admire your confidence," you say.

"Oh, really?"

"It takes balls of steel to tell a story like that with a straight face."

"Maybe I'm just super confident because I've actually seen all that."

You give me the smirk you reserve for your close guy friends, or girls you're really attracted to. A look acknowledging that the person you're talking to is particularly intelligent.

I put my foot on the first step of the wrought-iron staircase leading up to my place, then turn and say, "Want to come up?"

The street's totally empty. The air's perfectly still, not even the sound of a breeze. Behind you, a cat darts across the street.

"For real?"

You try not to look too excited, but you realize your face hurts from smiling.

"Yeah, for real."

"Okay, I'll come up."

"Are we sure we wanna do this?"

You tilt your head like a puppy. Then, with a playful look, you say, "Do what?"

"What we're about to do."

"What are we about to do?"

You come closer. Since I'm standing on the step, my face is exactly at the same height as yours. You catch a whiff of my fading perfume, but also a bit of my sweat from the party. Your head suddenly feels lighter. A tingle goes down your spine.

"You know what'll happen if you do this," I say.

You play innocent. "What'll happen?" you mutter.

"The story I told you."

Even though this should put a damper on your mood, it just makes you smile. "We sleep together and I win in the end," you say. "Seems like a pretty good deal to me. Anyway, I gotta check if you're bullshitting."

"I'm not bullshitting, I swear."

"What about you?" you ask. "Do you want to?"

"Want to what?"

You place your lips very gently against mine. A suspension of time, short but very sweet. Champagne fizzes in your ears. The muscles of your face tense up from smiling too long. You move your head back so you can see me better.

"To kiss me," you say.

I smirk, give a little nod. "What about the rest?" I ask.

"For the rest, it's on me," you say. "You warned me what I was getting into, so it's on me. If it ends badly, I swear, it's on me."

ACKNOWLEDGEMENTS

I'd like to thank Sophi Carrier, Rosalie Vaillancourt, and Laurianne Walker-Hanley for their help with research, as well as Suzie Bouchard for editing the jokes. I'd also like to thank my translator Neil Smith and designer Malcolm Sutton.

ABOUT THE AUTHOR

JEAN-PHILIPPE BARIL GUÉRARD is an actor and writer who lives in Montreal. He is the author of four novels: *Sports et divertissements* (published in English as *Sports and Pastimes*), *Royal* (winner of the Prix littéraire des collégiens), *Manuel de la vie sauvage* (which was translated into Spanish), and *Haute démolition* (*You Crushed It*). He also co-wrote *Les Cicatrisés de Saint-Sauvignac* with three other writers. Several of his books have been adapted for the stage and television, including *Royal*, *Haute démolition*, and *Manuel de la vie sauvage*. He also writes for the stage and screen.

PHOTO: KEVIN MILLET

ABOUT THE TRANSLATOR

NEIL SMITH is a writer and translator from Montreal. He has won the Hugh MacLennan Prize for Fiction and the Quebec Writers' Federation First Book Prize. He has also been nominated for the Governor General's Literary Award for Translation, the Sunburst Award, the Journey Prize, the Prix des libraires du Québec, and the Canadian Library Association Young Adult Book Award. His fiction has been translated into eight languages.

PHOTO: JULIE ARTACHO